Satan's Stones

Satan's Stones

by
Moniru Ravanipur

Edited with an Introduction by
M. R. Ghanoonparvar

University of Texas Press
Austin

Requests for permission to reproduce material from
this work should be sent to Permissions, University of
Texas Press, Box 7819, Austin, TX 78713-7819.

⊗The paper used in this publication meets the
minimum requirements of American National
Standard for Information Sciences—Permanence of
Paper for Printed Library Materials, ANSI Z39.48-1984.

Ravani'pur, Muniru.
    [Sang'ha-yi Shaytan. English]
    Satan's stones / by Moniru Ravanipur ; edited with an
introduction by M. R. Ghanoonparvar. — 1st ed.
        p.   cm.
    ISBN 0-292-77076-6 (pbk. : alk. paper)

    I. Ghanoonparvar, M. R. (Mohammad R.)   II. Title.
PK6561.R296S2613   1996
891'.5533—dc20   95-32498

Contents

Introduction

This collection is the translation of a volume of short stories by Moniru Ravanipur entitled *Sangha-ye Sheytan* (Satan's Stones), which is also the name of the title story of the collection. Perhaps the best-known contemporary Iranian writer among those who began their writing careers after the 1978–79 Islamic Revolution in Iran, Ravanipur is also one of the most prominent writers of Persian fiction today. *Sangha-ye Sheytan* was published first in January 1991 and went into a second printing only one month later. Five of the nine stories were in fact written in 1990–91 and are therefore representative of this important writer's recent work.

Moniru Ravanipur published her first book, *Kanizu*, also a collection of short stories, in late 1988. It was in 1989 with her first novel, *Ahl-e Gharq* (The Drowned), however, that she gained national recognition in Iran. *The Drowned*, which has been described by some critics as a novel of magical realism, introduced a new and innovative approach to Persian fiction writing, in terms of both style and structure as well as subject matter. In this novel, Ravanipur deals with beliefs and customs, superstitions, struggle for survival, and generally the lives of the inhabitants of a small fishing village called Jofreh on the Persian Gulf. Having been born and reared in this relatively isolated region, Ravanipur successfully renders the people of her childhood village and their lives in a tangible (though seemingly fantastic) fashion for her urban Iranian readers, for whom her characters may at first glance appear alien and exotic. Aside from its literary significance, *The Drowned* has also functioned to immortalize Ravanipur's childhood village, representative of hundreds of other small villages scattered throughout Iran. In fact, Jofreh's entire history spanned only a few decades: first established by a few families searching for a new place to settle, the village was soon devoured by the invasion of modernization and the expansion of nearby Bushehr Port and essentially disappeared.

Not all Ravanipur's works have dealt directly with Jofreh and her own childhood years. *Del-e Fulad* (Heart of Steel), which was published in 1990 and in which she engages in experimentation of style and novelistic technique, deals with the life of a woman writer in Tehran, her maturation as a woman and artist, the creative process, and the forces in her life that comprise and contribute to her creativity. This is also true of *Satan's Stones*, which, perhaps with the exception of the title story, displays Ravanipur's bold experimentation in narrative voice and technique and at the same time expands the horizons of her work in terms of subject matter and the creation of fascinating characters.

In the course of nearly a century since modern fiction writing began in Iran, and particularly in the period from post–World War II until the Islamic Revolution, the Persian fiction scene was dominated by male authors, who generally made their living in other professions, such as teaching. Although these authors took their writing very seriously, essentially their literary work occupied the place of a hobby in their lives. Among the various reasons behind this phenomenon were, of course, the lack of a sufficiently large readership and the existence of strict censorship. Moreover, because many writers were socio-politically engagé in their work, or were expected to be, and because women have generally been excluded from the public sphere, few women writers were given the opportunity to exercise their craft and gain deserved recognition for their work. Ravanipur is among a slowly growing number of authors in Iran who are now making their living through writing imaginative literature.

Despite the fact that more restrictions in terms of dress and access to certain positions have been imposed on women in postrevolutionary Iran, in the past decade an increasing number of women writers have distinguished themselves to the extent that today, among the country's dozen or so well-known novelists and short story writers, women occupy the most prominent positions. An important factor contributing to this new phenomenon is perhaps the success of these post-revolutionary women writers in not only liberating them-selves from the predominant male voice in Persian literature but also in finding their individual artistic focal point and style. This is certainly true of Moniru Ravanipur, who has established herself with her unique style and subject matter as well as her distinctive approach to the art of fiction. In a 1993 interview published in *Gardun* magazine, she speaks candidly about the process of her writing and her artistic and intellectual preoccupations. Concerning her travels to small villages throughout Iran where she gathers material for her work, she says:

> Different writers and artists work differently. Because I started my work by traveling, now it has become a neces-sary tool for me, like paper and pencil. . . . I have now come to the conclusion that it is impossible for me to stay in Tehran for two or three months away from the south-ern villages and be able to work. I am energized by them and new ideas form in my mind, events that are remote from those of cities. Here [Tehran], too, of course, has its own problems; for instance, there are strange suicides, a company is closed down, someone burns himself, another jumps off a high building. We must understand the roots of the problems that we face in the city. When you go back to the villages and learn about people's beliefs and myths, you realize that many incidents that occur in the city and the beliefs that have been transformed in the ur-ban environment have their roots in the villages.

In the villages Ravanipur visits frequently, and where con-ditions are often primitive, she is referred to as *chichika*, a term in local dialect that means "story woman." In the same interview, she describes an encounter in a small village with a woman giving birth:

They had laid the woman in labor down. Someone was sitting next to her and in the local dialect was saying: "If you are a girl, come out, we have two dresses, three veils, four bracelets, and two sets of earrings ready for you. If you are a boy, come out, we have a boat and much more for you." Then, every time the woman's labor pains would become more intense, they would add to the baby girl's dowry or the boy's possessions until eventually the boy had ten ships and the girl a house with a million toman's worth of clothes, etc. When the girl was born, the woman asked me to choose a name for her. I said: "Call her Golafruz." She said: "Alright, her name will be Golafruz; will you come for her wedding?" I said: "Yes, I will." Then I asked: "When should I come?" She said: "Nine or ten years from now, she will have her wedding, God willing, and you should come then." I said: "Fine."

A distinguishing feature of Ravanipur's work is the scenery and backdrop of her stories, which consists mainly of desert landscapes and remote regions of the country. To Ravanipur, the deserts of southern Iran are much more beautiful and a richer source of creative imagination for a literary artist than the green mountains and meadows of northern Iran near the Caspian Sea:

. . . To me Tehran is warm, but the heat is deadly; it is not a kind heat. I think in the south, even the fierce heat of the hot sun that burns everything is kind to me and possesses a special kind of beauty. When I was up north [by the Caspian Sea], after the first couple of days that I looked at the greenery, I was tired of it and put on my sunglasses, because I could not fathom the purpose of all that greenery. Water, wind, land, none of them can stimulate imagination. Even love, I think, depends on imagination. In other words, a human being creates love out of imagination rather than with the presence of something. I think it is the same in the south. People create memories. They have a mental predisposition for making up stories; they create the beauty that is absent and make their imagination active. For example, there is a tree in Bandar

Abbas [a port town on the Persian Gulf] called "Garum
Zangi" [Zanzibar *garum*], which is as pretty as its name.
At the side of the road, this tree is like an African woman
carrying something on her head, slender and shapely. Everything in the south has people in it, objects have life in
them, when you look at them, stories pour out of them.

In Ravanipur's latest collection of short stories, called *Siriya, Siriya,* and published in 1993, she draws on her first-
hand experiences in certain small islands in the north and
south of Iran. Having participated in the rituals of the people
of these remote areas, she also casts a critical look at their
beliefs and customs.

Satan's Stones is in many respects representative of Ravanipur's various endeavors as a writer of fiction. The title
story is reminiscent of *Siriya, Siriya* and to some extent even
The Drowned. Maryam, a young woman from a small village who has been studying medicine in the city, returns
home. By juxtaposing the old beliefs and superstitions with
modern science and education, Ravanipur presents aspects of
the cultural confusion and contradictions that exist throughout Iran. "My Blue Bird Is Dead," an experiment in symbolic
and psychological fiction, is a story about obsession, not only
that of the male character but also the woman narrator. From
a different perspective, it is also the story of a relationship
based on distrust.

"Love's Tragic Tale" reflects the evolution of man-woman,
guardian-ward relationships. By the end of the story, the relationship undergoes a transformation: the woman surpasses
the man as an artist but seems to have lost her identity as a
woman in the process of gaining it as an artist.

In "We Only Fear the Future" Ravanipur uses the plural
pronoun "we" as the narrative voice of a group of men ob-
sessed with a woman artist who has recently appeared in
their neighborhood. The men would like to know more about
her and perhaps meet her, but they are only capable of watching her from a distance. Ravanipur uses this odd relationship
as a vehicle for delving into a psychological and sociological
study of males of the human species and their perception of
females. While the story reflects the writer's own society, it

may also allude to a more universal phenomenon. Many allusions to art and its superficiality can also be read into this story, in addition to a commentary on the failure of men to understand (and indeed their general lack of interest in doing so) the females who make up their world.

Relationships between men and women in a more traditional sense are also the subject of the story of a professional dancer in "Jeyran." Although similar plots have been a favorite of other Iranian writers in the past, Ravanipur's skillful execution of Jeyran's dancing as a reflection of her emotional turmoil produces a unique short story (in fact, one of her favorites in the collection and her choice as the subject of the cover for the English edition). In the original Persian, the music of the language of the story corresponds to the movements of the dancer, a feature that is, regrettably, nearly impossible to reproduce in translation.

In "Haros," the question of identity is the central focus of the story of an Armenian family in postrevolutionary Iran and during the Iran-Iraq war. While every member of the family suffers the loss of friends in the war, a suffering shared by the whole society, and has a strong sense of belonging to the rest of the community, the story reveals, through the mother, the frustration of their alienation from others, reinforced by the neighbor's reiterated comment that ends the story: "Good for you, madame . . . you are different from us."

Recent reports from Iran indicate that this collection of stories has been banned by government authorities. Given the strict Islamic moral codes governing Iran today, it would not be farfetched to assume that the next story in the volume, "Play," may have contributed to the ban due to the story's frank references to the sexual relations between an unmarried couple. Nevertheless, like other stories in the volume, and somewhat reminiscent of "Love's Tragic Tale," "Play" also explores the attitude of men toward women and women's attempts to cope with this heretofore "man's world."

The Kafkaesque story "Another Version" is one of the most intriguing in the volume. It can be read as a symbolic story on several levels (political, social, and so on), but it can also be read as another account of a woman's life, from a different perspective, from birth to death, told elusively and humorously.

Finally, in "Three Pictures," which was a topical story when it was written in 1986, we follow a woman through her weekly ritual of visiting a cemetery where "martyrs" of the war, including the woman's husband, are buried as we witness her psychological effort in trying to cope with her grief.

In sum, the stories in this volume are fresh and innovative in style, subject matter, and technique and challenge us as readers to become active participants in the act of reading. And while they represent new, exciting trends in Persian fiction in recent years, they also reflect some of the concerns, particularly of women, in postrevolutionary Iran.

The translations are based on the second printing of *Sangha-ye Sheytan* (Tehran: Nashr-e Markaz, 1991) and are the result of the cooperative efforts of several young scholars who participated in my graduate translation seminar at the University of Texas at Austin in the spring of 1993. While "Satan's Stones," "My Blue Bird Is Dead," and "Another Version" are the result of the collaborative effort of all the translators whose names appear at the end of the stories, the rest were translated by the individual translators cited. In the fall of that year, Moniru Ravanipur visited Austin, during which time she read several stories in the English rendition and made specific comments about them. On behalf of all the translators and myself, I am most grateful to her. Special thanks go to Zjaleh Hajibashi; Dr. Ali Hossaini, Jr.; Persis Karim; and Diane Wilcox for reading the translations and offering valuable suggestions.

M. R. GHANOONPARVAR

SATAN'S STONES

Satan's Stones

To the dear memory of Mohammad Reza Rahimi, a bird of truth who flew from the grove of life

The sputtering red minibus let her off at the roadside and continued its way to the northern villages. A wind, biting and cold from the north, beat the desert sand against her face and legs. Sheltering her face with her hand, she huddled up and set out toward the village, shrinking away from a wind that whipped about her shoulders.

She passed through the large white Satan's stones that were scattered about for some distance around the village. No one knew in what distant time or with what enormous power Satan had thrown them into the desert. The shrieking of the wind swirled in her head, and a whirlwind seemed to be attacking the village. Like an old jinn with disheveled hair, it hid everything from view, a jinn who, with a voice unintelligible and frightening, sometimes calm and sometimes howling, was casting spells. Disheveled and demented, when the spells did not work, it threw dust and debris into the air.

As she remembered distant fairy tales of childhood, a smile rested on her lips, and to relieve her legs from the driving sand, she stood in the shelter of a rock and gazed toward the village. The whirlwind swirled around her and the rock, as though it did not want her to reach the village. Maybe it was strong enough to lift her and the rock and toss them somewhere far, far away, turning her into a rock—a white rock— and when a camel driver's children would pass it with their caravans, they would turn their faces away and, under their breaths, whisper a prayer.

She huddled against the rock and covered her ears tightly

so she could not hear the terrifying sound of the wind, so she would not know whose fate was being sealed, or whom the stones were entreating to restore their original forms. She thought of the days when she was no more than a child, when the wind would peep through the cracks in the windows and doors into the darkness of the room. Her mother would say:

"They are sighing. Satan's stones are sighing, and when they have atoned for all their sins, you will see that the desert is full of people—men and women."

She had come unannounced to make everyone happy. When she left, she didn't know it wasn't like school, that she could return six months later to this very village she loved, where she could stay for two weeks. How quickly the time had passed in Shiraz, with its paved streets and countless trees—here this road was still rocky, full of Satan's stones and the wailing of wind.

She peeked out from behind the rock. The whirlwind had released her and the rock. Disheveled, spouting spells, it had headed west. It did not seem to have accomplished anything.

She clutched her bag firmly. Passing through the white stones, she set out toward the village. A biting cold wind hit her face. The ground was frozen, and the uncommon chill of this mid-winter month had cracked the small stones. The wind blew into the palm grove near the village, and she could see the gnarled branches bending in every direction. *The old jinn goes to the middle of the palm grove sometimes. It tugs at the tresses of the palms so they won't give their crown of fruit to sinners during the date season, so that if they eat one, every single date they eat will ignite in their mouths.* She drew near to the first house—*still mud brick!*—with low doors and small windows whose frames were only big enough for a head, unlike those open windows in Shiraz . . . in houses and classrooms . . .

She looked at the blue door of a mud brick house and saw that it was still there—that very sign put on the door of Setareh's house at night. *A jinn who is the protector of the village smells sin, and at night it marks every house where the smell of sin is concentrated.* And who had ever seen this jinn?

Setareh, wearing a long orange dress, her black hair fallen over her breasts, with kohl-lined hazel eyes, opened the low blue door. It was as though she had been waiting for her, waiting for her, and maybe through a crack of a window, as always, guarding the rocky path.

Setareh's face lit up with a broad smile, and in the middle of the biting chill and the distant sound of the wind she cried: "Hello Maryam . . ."

Two years had passed since the jinn who watched over the village had seen the shadow of a heavy cloud over Setareh's house and appeared in the nanny's dream. The nanny had pointed to the sky in broad daylight with five henna-dyed fingers; there wasn't a single cloud. As punishment for loving a stranger, Setareh had been forced to come to this house—a house far from other houses. Two years ago, she had a house near the village square and lived with her mother. The stones that pelted the door and window of Setareh's house day and night, and the way the village women shunned her, drove her old mother to bed. Three days after the old woman's death, Gholam the Gendarme—who dropped by the village once every two months in a gendarmerie jeep—packed Setareh's things to take her to the city. Although she didn't love him, Setareh married him and settled down in this small mud brick house.

It had been a long time since Gholam the Gendarme had dropped by the village in the gendarmerie car for a ten-day stay. Setareh always stood behind the window—the closed window—and watched for the dust her husband raised in the distance as he came to the door.

Setareh's friendship and congeniality were evident in the glow on her face and the sound of her voice. But she seemed to be afraid that someone would see her—see her talking with Maryam. She did not come out of the doorway; she stood right there, both hands on the doorpost, and smiled.

"Hello, Setareh! How are you? How is your son?"

"He's fine, kind of you to ask—but how about you? How have you been?"

She was in a good mood, but she watched everything around her. She was afraid that the village nanny would see her, the nanny who smelled everything and seemed to be everywhere. How many times had the women been forced to sit in the village square and ululate toward Setareh's house? Even Mother had gone; they had taken her by force.

"Are you finished with school?"

"No, Setareh, it doesn't end that fast. It will take eight years."

"Eight years is a whole lifetime . . ."

Setareh had not gone into the village for a long time. Every Thursday she went around the mud brick houses to reach the graveyard and say a prayer over the graves of her dead. If it weren't for Gholam the Gendarme with his rifle, and the bullets he had fired in the village square, the nanny could very well have had her paraded naked through the streets in front of everyone; she could have had her long black hair shaved off.

No one wanted to confront the nanny. It was she who had advised Mother not to send Maryam to the port city. Mother had said:

"She's not going to a strange place—it's her uncle's house."

If it weren't for her uncle, who had lived in the city since his return from military duty and taken a wife from the port city where his children were educated, Maryam would never have been able to go to the port city and then to Shiraz . . .

Setareh's eyes sparkled. She leaned her arm, covered with bracelets, against the door and seemed to be searching for something to keep Maryam, to draw her toward the house. And if she went into the house? She was frightened. She looked all around her. No one was there—only the whistling wind blowing dust and debris.

After a long time, Maryam's uncle had come to the village with a bundle of souvenirs to talk with the nanny; her eyes had gleamed. Mother gave her lunch every day, and the other houses hosted the nanny every day, to ensure that food would remain plentiful on their tables; that, with the nanny's blessing, no one would get sick; that the rain would fall on time; and that the dead would rest in their graves.

She had to leave. She had to break off this familiar, friendly exchange. She said good-bye and set off. The soles of her feet were freezing. A rough, abrasive wind beat against her face. A cow mooed from a distance. She had wasted too much time. She should not have stayed so long . . . Now she wanted to get home faster, to sit in a warm room beside a brazier full of charcoal and listen to the sound of a potato baking in the coals.

She reached the village square. The cold had blackened the familiar old tamarisk, and the tall narrow trunk of a palm with no top sank into the ground like an iron post on the left side of the square. The barefoot children rode stick horses made of palm tree branches, their cheeks red and their noses running. In a corner of the square, a small whirlwind played with dust and debris.

As she came nearer, the children stopped playing one by one and stared at her. She stretched out her hand to pat a little boy on the head. The little boy ran, and the others backed away on their wooden horses. A window facing the square opened, a woman put her head out and called:

"Sardar, Sardar, come home . . ."

Maryam waved at the woman. She saw the woman's frozen, disgusted look, saw her back into the house and slam the window shutters closed. Maryam was stunned. It was Zoleykha. Why didn't she acknowledge her greeting? Maryam saw two other windows open, saw frowning women call their sons, look at her sourly, and slam the shutters.

This is where she used to play. Her childhood years in this very square. And now she stood in the middle of the square, amid frowning and closed windows. The children had run away, and the disgusted glare of the women remained in the square. Someone had certainly seen her talking and laughing with Setareh, a woman who had gotten pregnant by a stranger. She saw that they were watching her between the cracks behind closed windows. She was cold, and the whirlwind from the square was swirling around her legs, straining as if to lift her and carry her away, carry her where . . . Where would it toss her?

She smiled faintly. She could say that Setareh had blocked her way, that her little boy was ill, that it was only hello, how are you; she could talk to her mother, and she could say . . . Say what? What could she say?

She went on her way. The wind blew dried bits of dung along the ground. She hunched over, face to face with the wind. This cold had a nasty bite. The chill ran through her bones; it was different from the cold weather in Shiraz, where it drizzled continuously and you wanted to walk in the street under the tall cypresses, where snowflakes fell softly on your face without getting you all wet, and the squares were all green, with tall water fountains and houses with big, bright windows . . . How far away that city was . . . how far.

The tap-tapping sound of a hand patting bread onto the walls of a kiln sent a pleasant warmth through her veins. She was in the village—the smell of fresh bread and a cow that mooed and a kiln around which women were gathering, waiting for a turn.

She saw the kiln from a distance, and the gathering of village women, and the nanny with her eternally black clothes, who was sitting over the kiln. She always wore black and she was always alone . . . the old virgin of the village . . . Mother used to say: She devoted herself to the people, to the village. It went back many years to the time when tuberculosis had struck the village and a black hungry jinn had come from who knows where and was eating the flesh and blood of men. So the jinn would let the village alone, the nanny, who was fourteen years old in those days, sat before a water bowl. With an incantation that the nanny before her had chanted, she saw and heard in the bowl of water that a fourteen-year-old girl must remain a virgin forever, so she did, and the black jinn turned white and harmless and stayed right there in the air of the village so he could prevent anyone from getting close to the nanny.

A round wooden bowl full of bread sat beside the nanny. Everyone gave her their first loaf of baked bread. Maryam sped up. She saw wooden trays of dough beside women waiting their turn, and women who had seen her turned around one by one and watched her.

Before she reached the tall familiar bread kiln, she said: "Hello . . ."

The women kept their eyes on the nanny's face, some of them shifted in discomfort, and they said softly, under their breath:

"Hello . . ."

The nanny, with sharp pursed lips and a look that pierced

like a drill, stared into Maryam's eyes. Her tattooed hairless
eyebrows were raised. The green star on her chin twitched as
if talking to itself. Two red ringlets were affixed to her hard,
bony temples. From underneath her black veil, her long thin
hair, like red bloody snakes, stretched to the ground.

Maryam collected herself under the nanny's hard and heavy
gaze. For a moment she remained confused, saw the nanny
give a woman a threatening hand gesture, and heard her say:
"What's with you? Why are you so dumbstruck? Did you
see the Virgin Mary or something?"

She saw the nanny's sneer, saw the woman who gave her a
ball of dough. The nanny's wrinkled brown hands patted out
the dough. The other women drew their veils over their faces
and busied themselves with their work. From the corners of
their eyes, they watched her leave.

She had gone a few steps when she heard the dry sound of
the nanny's ululation, which ricocheted off her back like a
whip. Cold as ice, horror ran through her soul, and she heard
the women's small titters, as if they were laughing at Setareh.

Under the heavy stares of the women, Maryam retreated
into an alley, an old familiar alley that seemed to have become even narrower and darker with the winter's cold. She
leaned against a wall. She closed her eyes and opened them
an instant later, terrified. She feared that the walls would
come forward and crush her. She shook her head vehemently,
and then, at the thought of the distant city with its tall cy-
press trees, a faint smile appeared on her face.

She continued and came to another alley. The doors to
the houses were open, with elk and deer horns mounted
over them, symbols to drive away any calamity or disas-
ter. It would take eight more years to become a doctor,
and then she would return to the village, and maybe she
could patiently remove these talismans one by one from the
houses . . . She would open a place and get help from the girls
in the village . . . She had seen what the nanny had done with
the woman next door. Five years ago, when the woman had
gone into labor, the nanny had waved the branch of a date
palm that she had lit in the brazier. She had waved it through
the air in the room so that the jinn who threatens women in
childbirth would let go of the woman's liver. She had seen the

woman lose her voice in pain and beg, her body convulsing, that salt be poured on the fire again. She had seen the nanny, at the cry of the baby, cram a fistful of burning cow dung between the legs of the woman and she had heard the cries of the woman.

From the bend in the alley, she saw their house, which had antlers mounted over the door, which, as usual, was open . . . Her gaze slid down the door and she took a deep breath. It seemed as though the door had been freshly painted, blue. She smiled, seeing a rooster perched on the low courtyard wall, and a chicken pecking the ground next to the wall lifted its head up for the rooster.

She went through the courtyard door. The whole place was unkept and disorderly. Chicken droppings and dried-up dung were scattered everywhere. She saw her mother bent over the well drawing water. She was preoccupied. Her profile was thin and gaunt. Maryam walked quickly toward the well and said excitedly:

"Hello . . . Mama."

Mother shook her head vehemently, as if to drive away a hallucination, but a moment later she turned back and straightened, joy lighting up her face. She dried her hands on the hem of her petticoat and suddenly paused in hesitation. Maryam ran toward her and saw the stinging bitterness in her face. Stunned and tired, she looked at her, not knowing what to do.

"How are you, Mama? Y-you're not feeling well."

Maryam threw her arms around Mother's neck and kissed her. Mother drew back slowly, imperceptibly, and asked hoarsely:

"When did you get here?"

"Now, just now."

Mother took her bag:

"It's a good thing you came . . . very good."

She seemed to be talking to herself. Maryam looked at her. Her hair had turned completely white; her thin, sad lips were pressed together. They went toward the room together.

"Mama, has something happened in the village?"

"No . . . why do you ask?"

Mother's voice was hoarse and rusty. She wouldn't look

at Maryam. She was listening to the sounds outside. She seemed to be apprehensive. They reached the room. Mother put the bag in a corner, sat beside the brazier, and pushed back the ashes in it with some tongs. She seemed to be keeping busy so she wouldn't have to say or hear anything. The silence began to make Maryam anxious.

"Is there fighting in the village?"

Mother emptied a tin of charcoal into the brazier. She put a glowing ember on the charcoal and started fanning it.

"No, what fighting?"

She was evasive and reticent in her answers. Maryam wanted to say the nanny had ululated, but she could not; sweat broke out on her brow. She was embarrassed. Mother pursed her lips and lit the charcoal in the brazier.

"How long will you be here, dear?"

"Two weeks."

"Good . . . very good."

Mother heaved a long sigh. She was looking down and stoking the fire with the tongs. Maryam stood up and went toward her. She put her arms around her neck and kissed her on the forehead:

"Are you sad, Mama?"

Mother forced a bitter smile.

"No, thank God, nothing is wrong with me."

"Then what happened? Where did Akbar go?"

"Akbar . . . he has gone to the mill . . ."

Maryam took her mother's face in her hands and looked her straight in the eyes.

"Mama, what is it?"

Mother's lips quivered; her eyes welled with tears and in between sobs she entreated:

"Is it . . . is it really you?"

Maryam's hands went limp. She let go of her mother and said with surprise:

"Of course it's me . . . who else could I be?"

Mother, who was now sobbing, grabbed her shoulders and entreated:

"You mean, nothing . . . nothing's changed?"

"Well, what could have changed, dear?"

The gate creaked. Maryam saw the nanny, who had come

into the yard. Behind her were the village women and the children who had suddenly appeared. Mother stood helplessly, kissed Maryam and said:

"It's nothing, it's nothing."

The nanny was standing in the door frame, with one hand on the door and one hand on her hip. She smirked. Mother was now standing up.

"She's pure . . . my daughter is as pure as the Koran."

"Well, now, we've got the thief and the stolen goods; we'll test it out."

Maryam was leaning against the wall. The room had grown dark. The village women, with heads of a thousand serpents, were peeping over the nanny's shoulder . . . Mother said with a sob:

"It is a lie . . . it's a lie . . ."

The nanny stepped forward, entered the room, and said:

"It doesn't lie, don't speak blasphemy . . . don't make your dead turn over in their graves."

Mother quietly swallowed her sobs. The nanny came closer and gestured at Maryam with her brown, thin hands:

"Get up . . ."

Maryam looked with terror at her mother. Mother grabbed the nanny's skirt, pleading:

"Right here in the room is better . . . out there is indecent; they'll see."

The nanny's smirk widened:

"More indecent is that in that city of strangers she has disgraced everyone."

A thousand bulging black eyes watched Maryam, and in the midst of the hot breaths and the gaping mouths of the entire village, she heard her mother's voice:

"Wait till her brother comes . . . he has gone to Shiraz to pick her up . . . wait till he comes."

The black bulging eyes were getting close. A thousand hands were reaching for her, and Maryam saw the two brown snakes that coiled around her arms and other snakes that grabbed her feet and lifted her. Something like a chunk of stone was caught in her throat and was stifling her scream.

She shook her head vehemently. A hand grabbed her hair

and pulled . . . She was over the water cellar and saw that the children, big and small, were standing on the mud brick walls. The air was full of noise, and noises were whistling past her head, wrapping around her neck, and she couldn't breathe.

"It has appeared in the nanny's dream three times."

"I saw it too. I saw that it was turning black as before; then I heard it say, it is the fault of the girl who is away from here."

Her body burned, as if a thousand snakes were biting her, as though she were caught between thousands of Satan's stones, stones that were moving toward her, rolling over her, crushing her arms and legs and her whole body.

A hand laid her on the ground. Two old women grabbed her legs and pulled them forcefully toward themselves. Some women sat on her legs; her hands were pinned to the ground, and two hands were holding her head. Her legs were spread open. A woman was handing the nanny an egg. The nanny was standing in front of her. Maryam's eyes were burning, she could hear the voices:

"Not even a single tear."

"Her unfortunate father is shuddering in his grave."

The village was full of bulging eyes. The old nanny was sitting and groping her legs with her hands. Some hands spread her legs apart. The nanny's sleeves were pulled up. Her eyes were continuously opening and closing.

"Move over, dear, let me see what I'm doing."

"She's right, it's dark . . . move back."

The lump of stone in her throat had grown bigger. A brown snake was moving between her legs. She couldn't feel the weight of the Satan's stones on her arms and legs. The world had turned into the shape of a small egg, and her leg was trembling from the egg touching it. It seemed as though an insect was jumping up and down there. A raspy snort came out of her mouth. It was the sound of a chicken's gasp, one whose throat had been cut. She shook herself and a strange scream emerged from her throat.

"Oh, God."

The women pulled back. Nanny ordered: "Hold her tight." And again she pushed the egg. The women were watching quietly. She saw the nanny's long finger, which was like a snake, twisting in the middle of her petticoat. Nanny was cleaning her finger.

"Oil."

She felt the nanny's slippery, cold finger between her legs. She had become soaking wet with sweat. She was cold and shivering. When the nanny raised her finger, her face shone and her eyes sparkled. The women, with their eyes glued to her mouth, remained silent. The nanny patiently shook her hand toward the palm trees where the old jinn lived and said:

"Thanks."

The sound of ululating resonated through the village. A woman emptied a sugar bowl on her head. Mother had fainted in the women's arms. Maryam was watching with glazed eyes. The old nanny came forward with her oily hand and kissed Maryam, who lay motionless, and said:

"Doctor, you make your mother proud, you bring pride to your village."

Maryam could hear nothing but the sound of the wind that had been ricocheting between the Satan's stones.

MAY—JUNE 1990

SHIRAZ

TRANSLATED BY PERSIS KARIM, ATOOSA KOUROSH, PARICHEHR
MOIN, DYLAN OEHLER-STRICKLIN, REZA SHIRAZI, AND
CATHERINE WILLIAMSON

My Blue Bird Is Dead

Now you say he was innocent, and you knew him, knew that he wandered around in the streets every day looking for me, with those scrawny shoulders, that low forehead, and those two eyes I'm sure were filled with the corpses of dead birds . . . but I know he killed them himself, and I am certain that he was accustomed to it . . . people like him don't show themselves to people like you, who are their friends. They don't show their hand. You have to be a woman to smell it and know, and I was, I am, even now I am, and I can smell it. Now, six years have passed since '84, and in '84 six years had passed since . . . I guess '78 . . . my blue bird had died. No, God, what am I saying? It was frozen, that is, it had thawed. It had taken six years for it to thaw, and I knew that little by little it would dry up and the smell would permeate everywhere, and then, what do you think would sit on a dead corpse, even if it is a blue bird? Weariness—weary of seeing the flies, hearing the buzzing of their black wings, and not love, would you believe that it was not love; if you only believe this I will be satisfied—yes, it was weariness that drew me there. After all, how long can a green bird sing in a cage alone? If it sings at all . . .

   That's why I picked up my green bird and left the house. I thought, I must find a mate for him, so he'll sing. I saw him in the square. He was crouched over, curled up inside himself, and like all people who are afraid of something, he watched everything around him. He was wearing a brown overcoat, and he had clenched his hand into a fist inside his pocket. I said, his green bird must have frozen. I sped up so

I'd get there faster, faster than he, so I could tell the bird seller, I got there too late, and he was just showing off his blue bird. In the middle of all those singing birds, I opened my hand and showed him my green bird. That's when he told me:

"Come on, take this blue one, or give me the green one . . ."

That's how I met him, and he quickly—very quickly—figured out how my blue bird had frozen . . . but he said it was dead . . . That very day, on our way to his house, he said: He's dead. I said: He's just now dying. First he was frozen. He said: No, he was dead from the beginning. I said: He sings. He said: Don't the dead sing? And then, when we came to his street, he said:

"But my green birds escape—they don't die."

At this point I began to have doubts. He had said: "My green birds . . ." He'd used the plural. He'd said it was already dead from the beginning, and he knew the dead sing, too—meaning that until the needle reaches their hearts, they sing. And then he'd laughed a childlike laugh that distracted you so you wouldn't look into his eyes. But when he put the key in the door, I looked, and I saw. I went just for this, to draw the corpses of dead birds out of his eyes one by one and shake them in front of his face. I thought, let me prove, at least to this one, that he himself is the killer, that he is used to killing . . . but he knew his role well. That is why he had cleaned up the cage, put my green bird beside his blue bird, whistled loudly, and said:

"This one won't escape, surely it won't . . ."

It was obvious that he was planning how to push a small sharp needle next to my green bird's heart and then to sit and watch the spectacle, the spectacle of hearing the moans that ever so slowly, over the course of six years, grow silent and then decompose . . . You want to know how the moans of a green bird decompose, don't you? Haven't you smelled it? Fine, but you must know I'm a woman and I can smell these things, like that day, the first day I went to his house and I knew the smell of carcasses, and when he looked at me with a smile, I said:

"Don't ever do that again . . ."

He said:

"Do what . . . ?"

I didn't say a word, but I knew he wanted to draw it out of me. I didn't say a word that day, but later I said . . . You pierced a needle near its heart so it wouldn't die. It wouldn't die right away, you wanted to drag it out so that you could savor the taste in your mouth . . . He said: "My God, what wild ideas . . . what has that man done to you? . . . My God." He had wanted me to bring everything to his house, a water bowl, the perch my green bird sometimes sat on, and where it sang when it felt like it, and a lot of other things . . . I brought them, not that I didn't know his plan . . . it was as clear as day to me. I had seen the carcasses of birds in his eyes, but I said if I were close to him, the sooner he would begin and the sooner I would catch him in the act . . . after all, the feathers of dead birds were all over his hands. His hands still smelled of carcasses . . .

But there was one thing that was different from 1978 . . . he had patience, he moved forward slowly, and if I had waited, it would have dragged on for a hundred years . . . so I said: "I am going. Let the birds stay in the cage. We will visit each other once in a while, and sometimes I will come here and listen to them sing . . ."

When I said this he looked at me; I saw his mouth twitching. It was as if he understood that I had understood. Then he said:

"What singing . . . what singing?"

And I left. I was in my own house again, the same place that we passed yesterday in the car. One day I will take you there so you can see I am telling the truth. Even now that smell lingers in my house. Even if I open the doors and windows, it does not help . . . because he kept coming over so often. Finally I could not stand it anymore; one day I went over to his house. I knew he was not there and he was on his way to my house. I left a note for him. I wrote:

"Don't come over anymore; you can call me on the telephone; this way they will live longer . . ."

I wanted him to reveal himself as soon as possible, to carry out his plan. I was at the end of my rope, and on that very day he came over at sunset.

He said:

"It is an excuse."
I said:
"No, I just want them to live . . ."
He said:
"Let me come once a month."
I said:
"No."
He said:
"They'll freeze, I am frozen."
The last time he came, the time before the last time I saw him, it was late at night. He was banging against the walls and his mouth . . . ugh, it smelled like a thousand dead birds. I threw him out. It was snowing. He stood in the snow in front of the glass window, stubborn and obstinate as always. I turned off the light and could see it was snowing and he was standing there. He stood there till morning. Until I drew open the curtain and saw that a snowman was standing in front of my window. When I drew open the curtain, he moved and snow fell from his body. With difficulty, he dragged himself out of the snow and started walking. I heard his dry cough. The next day when I went there I thought he must be frozen now and wondered how long it would take him to thaw out . . . but he was sitting with his knees stuck up to his chest, as if waiting. He was coughing. The same dry cough. He was laughing the same kind of laugh I mentioned. And I was afraid to look to the left above his desk. There, he had to do it right there. I had told him:
"You'll probably kill this green bird one day and pin it on the wall above your desk, like a dried-up butterfly."
I knew he had done this many times before, that was why I was afraid, I wanted to see and I wanted not to see, to hear and not to hear. But with those laughs that followed his long dry coughs and his raspy voice that sounded as if it were saying, I have a fever, I have a fever, he asked:
"When will you go to the bird shop next? How many years from now?"
I said:
"Don't you want to understand . . . ?"
He said:
"You're used to it . . . you're used to it."

I said:

"Smell it, just smell it."

He said:

"Every time you come, there's this smell."

I said:

"In your eyes, it comes from there."

It was then that he grabbed my chin with his hot, feverish hand and pulled it toward him and said:

"In your pocket, the left side, put your hand in your overcoat pocket . . ."

I put my hand in it. It was the carcass of a blue bird. It was his own doing. Probably when I had turned my head to look at the corner of his desk, he had put it there. He had made a mistake. He'd killed the wrong one . . . and then all I could do was take my green bird and escape.

And what you're telling me, that he was looking for me for some time, even until this last year when I was traveling and had made myself a wanderer so I could forget how slyly he killed my blue bird. It's nothing new. It was the same in '78. And he, whom you don't know at all, constantly followed me, in the streets . . . like a murderer whose thoughts and imagination draw him to the scene of the crime . . . Both of them were like this and perhaps he wanted to know what I would do and how I would moan. You know, he would push the needle in next to their hearts so it wouldn't touch their hearts and then would sit in silence to watch them flutter.

And then I even showed him one day, I showed him how he pushed the needle, and then I put the bird in the cage, the blue bird, and the bird, like this . . . like this, look at me, was panting like this, fluttering and moaning. I said:

"You do something that gradually makes their moaning peak and then, silence . . ."

He would say:

"Don't say it, don't say I freeze them; I can't, that's not my doing."

And then, like you, like you who are frowning, he would close his eyes. He would say:

"You don't want to see how it struggles . . . in the throes of death."

He said:

"I don't want to see you."
And you know . . . now I . . . my green bird is lonely. And
how long do you think a lonely green bird can sing in a
cage—if it sings at all—and on a corpse, even if it were a
blue bird, what would sit on it? And this weariness . . .
weariness . . . and how can you say that it's not his doing? It
was not his doing. Why have you been clenching your fist in
your pocket? And this . . . what is it in your pocket that's
squirming . . . ? Is your blue bird lonely? Lonely?

16 DECEMBER 1990
TRANSLATED BY PERSIS KARIM, ATOOSA KOUROSH, PARICHEHR
MOIN, DYLAN OEHLER-STRICKLIN, REZA SHIRAZI, AND
CATHERINE WILLIAMSON

Love's Tragic Tale

Sa'di is not man enough to play chess with you in the game of love.

This is love's tragic tale. A tale that will be repeated as long as the crystal ball of time exists, so long as this crystal ball doesn't crash into a planet or a star from another time and break; in the end time may explode from within because of these same tragic love stories that are repeated and fill its limits; and when time is filled to capacity with emotions, with stifled disappointments and solitudes that cry out, its crystal shell will shatter . . . but each love story surely makes a place for itself in the scattered atoms of this crystal ball and itself creates a new "time," and perhaps the day will come when eternity and that which is created and that which is not will be nothing but crystal atoms of time that have a seed of love from the tragic tale of love in their hearts. And then time will be a woman and a man asleep in a bubble of time or some stories with endings not quite the same . . .

Because of this story, many people know the woman now, and to mention her name would not really change anything, a woman who wrote her own story in stories. And there is a man, too, whose existence or nonexistence is all the same, because no one knows him. And how they came to know each other . . . this isn't all that important either. When a story wants to take shape, it finds its own path. Finding a job, reading a story, publishing a book, it doesn't really make a difference . . .

The woman was simple. There wasn't any gap between her mind, her mouth, and her heart. Her words were the same as her thoughts and feelings, and in matters of love she didn't really believe in time. She was always in love and she wasn't one of those people who are in love one minute and then forget . . .

So, the first time she saw the man she said:

"You're very handsome, come, let's be friends . . . I'm very lonely."

The man was sitting at the table with disheveled hair and a stubble on his face, he was eyeing her, a slight smile on his lips. The woman's movements and mannerisms were such that his only thought was that she was nothing more than a child and he could mold her into a novelist.

The man had read the woman's stories and pretended that he was interested in her work and said the things he should say, and without mentioning a word about love the woman understood that if she wrote good stories she could make the man her own.

The days were passing and the man had his faint smile and with that smile he would leave everything conditional and up in the air. The woman was the way she was. She paced inside the room, went through books and the library; she spread out all the papers on the table, gathered them up, spread them again . . .

There was restlessness in the woman's every step and word, and one day when she had messed up the whole place she sat facing the man and said:

"Give me your hand so I can tell your fortune."

The man said:

"Save it for when you become a writer . . ."

The woman said:

"But I want to take your hand and stroke my hair."

The man laughed and asked:

"Why?"

The woman said:

"I want to caress my hair with your hand."

The man laughed and said:

"Crazy."

But he didn't give her his hand.

I'm writing this story quickly because I'm afraid someone will come in, sit in that chair next to the window, look at me, and ask: How's your work coming? I'm writing this story far from everyone's gaze; I don't want people to read it before it's finished. That's why I haven't even specified the locations, because naming the places, cities, and buildings not only takes time, which is exactly what I don't have, it also doesn't solve anything, and it's enough just to know that all of these events have occurred in the crystal ball of time.

And time for a woman like her, who was after someone to love her, this was the only meaning time had, and she didn't see any difference between one second and one year, and no matter where she was, she drew out the essence of time so that she could reach it, reach that moment when she would see him as a man, see herself as a woman, and see nothing else.

That's how she began her work. As though she got help from her very being so that she could breathe life into words. It was as though the words were torn from her body and soul, molecule by molecule. She wrote every day, one story after another, all of them love stories. There was also the man who read the stories, nodded his head, and was satisfied with his own work.

Sometimes the woman would read a story she had finished for the man and then she would say:

"I'm tired. Come on, let's go for a walk."

The man would shake his head with a smile and the woman knew that the time still hadn't come for the man to appear in public shoulder to shoulder with her. She understood the distance; she doubted her work. She went on reading and writing.

Time passed and the woman's books were published one after another. And the man was spending all his time reading her books, and every day he was more and more absorbed by her, or, to tell the truth, absorbed by the heroine of her stories. The man would go and sit in the woman's room and the woman would flit from one thing to another. For a long time she had been speaking chaotically and confusedly and this condition grew more pronounced every day, reaching a point at which the man couldn't figure out when the heroine of the woman's stories was speaking and when the woman herself was speaking. The refrain of all the woman's words had become:

"Do you love me?"

The man always smiled and answered:

"How's your work coming?"

And suddenly she would understand, collect herself, and show her hand to the man, where there was a mark left by a pen. It had become calloused, and the man said:

"Well, that's what happens when you work . . ."

And the woman would get back to her work again. How long had it been, how much time, until those changes gradually settled into the woman's body and soul? A woman who in the beginning wanted with her whole being for the man to come and read her stories, and who later was afraid for the door to open and for someone to come in and bend over a page blackened with words.

Time in the woman's life was never important, if a seed was planted, a seed of love, nothing could cross or scratch it out; but the man was gradually realizing that the woman didn't show any enthusiasm. If he called her, she would slowly turn her head toward him as though she were thoroughly immersed in what she was writing. Her look no longer had that loving sparkle and childlike eagerness, even though the heroine in her stories had eyes that sparkled. She had a loving look and her behavior and actions became more and more enthusiastic and childlike.

And the man read the stories every day, before and after publication. He knew the woman better and better, a woman whose flesh and blood he could feel in her stories.

So that the woman would write more and so that the atmosphere of her stories would continue to be romantic, the man played music for her, and he would squeeze fresh fruit for her so that the movements of her head and neck wouldn't be so sluggish. He would attend to her with food and drink, but the woman paid no attention to his kindness, she just wrote. One day when the man said, "You're tired, let's take a walk," the woman replied with a soft voice and a fixed and nebulous gaze:

"I can't, I have work to do."

And she did not go. The woman did not pay attention to reviews or journals. Journals that were all in competition with each other to talk about her. She did not know in what numbers her books were published. When the man enthusiastically stood facing her with the newspaper in his hand, she did not show the slightest reaction. Day by day her movements became more sluggish.

One day when the man got up from bed, he laughed to himself. He had never laughed like this, especially to himself. He had a strange feeling. He was remembering the woman's playfulness, the childlike mannerisms she had, and the repetitive refrain she used to say in the beginning:

"Do you love me?"

The man was singing to himself and he was being drawn toward the woman, and finally he went to a flower shop, bought a flower, and set off. The woman was, as always, busy writing. It was as if she were writing the last words of a story and only her hand was moving and her whole body was like a stone statue. She was distant from everything, even time, and it seemed as if she was just a hand hastily writing. The man put the flower that he had brought in a vase and set it before her. The woman did not look. She was transfixed on what she was writing. Her eyelids weren't even blinking. It was as if she had reached the final sentence. The man saw that she had concluded the sentence with a period, and her hand stayed still, just as it was, on top of the page she had just written. The man slowly took the pages out from under her hand. He read the title of the story: Love's Tragic Tale. He laughed. He tapped the woman's shoulder, looked at her face, and was baffled. The woman wasn't the woman any longer. She was a fossil made of words and the man tapped her shoulder so that he could be sure, and suddenly thousands of words scattered on the ground, and among those thousands of words, the man saw these . . .

"You're so handsome . . . come, be my friend, I'm very lonely."

29 DECEMBER 1990
TEHRAN
TRANSLATED BY CATHERINE WILLIAMSON

We Only Fear the Future

We were poets, and had no memories. Every afternoon from around four o'clock we would stand on that street in front of the bookstore talking, reciting poetry, and arguing. It was the same every day. Words weren't real anymore; they just followed us like a swarm of flies, buzzing and flying over our heads until we reached the bookstore. Then, if we got tired, there was a teahouse by the bookstore where we would sit and drink tea—and again the sound of buzzing flies would resonate through the teahouse, until our jaws got tired and we left.

There was a row of shops with apartments above them across from the bookstore on the other side of the street. We had never been aware of the apartments until the day we saw them.

It might have been a Saturday. I say "might" because suddenly we were all confused, and to this day, we don't know which day it was and which day it wasn't. But we all know this: she hadn't been there before. Not in the apartment above the shop across the street, which had a little door that opened onto the street—the door we had just seen—and not even in the city. Had there been a woman like that in so small a city, we would certainly have known. We were searching for a memory; we were poets, and none of us had a memory of a woman dressed all in black, who didn't tie her black scarf, so the whiteness of her neck was visible sometimes, but not always. We knew this from each other's flashing looks. Our eyes sparkled that day, those days . . .

It was four o'clock the first time she came out of her house.

She had an oval face, narrow, compressed lips, and black hair that was probably long; if it had been loose, it would have reached her waist. There was a cloud of sadness over her face, and we thought that since she was all in black maybe she was grieving, and we grieved too.

When she came across the street and went into the bookstore, her head and neck moving gracefully as she watched the cars, it suddenly occurred to us that we needed to take a look at the books; perhaps a new one had come in. No matter that we hadn't read a book in a long time, or been inside the bookstore. That's where we thought she wanted the works of Van Gogh. We had become disoriented by her voice, and we weren't listening anymore. It wasn't clear if we had listened to begin with. Only words, bright transparent words, hovered in the air, and we concluded that she was an artist, and wanted to buy an easel, paints, and a canvas.

When she left, the bookstore was empty. We no longer had anything to keep us there, and we went outside. But it seemed as though we didn't know why we used to always stand there, or what we talked about.

That same day, from a distance, we thought we saw the little door open again. A moment later we had just noticed the apartment's curtains, which were faded. We guessed that it must be a big room, since big rooms have big glass doors; she had probably made that place her studio. It faced the street, and it filled with light when the sun rose. And you have to have light to paint.

When we came the next day, we saw that a new curtain was hanging up—a curtain with seagulls all over it, seagulls that had lost their way, had strayed far from the sea, and didn't know which way to go now. Their heads and necks moved as if they were asking their way of us; they seemed to want us to show them the way to the sea. That's why we talked about seagulls and then crowded into the bookstore to see what books they had about the sea and seagulls. We wanted to find out how seagulls find their way; we wanted to know and be reassured.

It was a week before we talked about anything besides the sea and seagulls, and afterward our business took us elsewhere. Perhaps if the curtain hadn't been a little too short, if we hadn't been able to see her calves and know she was sitting facing the street, perhaps we would have kept on talking about seagulls. But when we came on the eighth day we saw her sitting there, and we knew she was facing the street, because we could see the hem of her black skirt, which reached her calves. Every now and then we saw a hand pick up something off the floor, and we knew that her paintbrush must have fallen, or a tube of paint, or one of her sketching pencils . . .

We left that day when it got dark, and our calves hurt until morning. The next day we all came earlier, and she wasn't there. She wasn't there, but at exactly a quarter to three we saw her legs. She came and sat down, adjusted the chair a little, and got to work. Her pencil or brush fell two or three times . . . we saw her hand, too, so sweet and white.

We stood there like that for ten days and watched. No one knew what she was drawing, but we always watched in case the curtain should move, and it did. From then on, we came every day at a quarter to three and stood by the bookstore. Sometimes we would go out of our way to come early so we could drink tea in the teahouse. The flavor of the tea there had really changed; no one drank tea at home anymore. At exactly sixteen minutes to three, we would leave the teahouse and stand where we were supposed to stand.

That day she pulled the curtain aside. The eleventh day. We saw her take the painting from the easel, put another canvas on it, and sit down without closing the curtain. We looked at each other in disbelief, our eyes sparkling, as if we had been relieved of a terrible torment. We took deep breaths and watched that place from the corners of our eyes, pretending that we weren't even aware of her. We saw that sometimes she pulled back from the canvas, and sometimes came close . . . we knew she was looking outside, and we were sure she was drawing one of us.

That's why our movements became repetitive, and we did the same thing every day. We thought that if she'd painted to a certain point the day before, say to where one of us had waved his hand, we had to repeat those very movements so she could finish her painting.

Because we didn't know anything about painting—how

long it takes to draw a sketch or how a painting on an easel comes to life—we went to the bookstore and bought all the books on learning to paint, painting, and the biographies of the great artists. We read them and were somewhat reassured. Only one thing tormented us: our hair had grown so long, and we were growing beards. It wasn't our fault; we always tried to keep everything under control. Every once in a while we would be preoccupied with this problem, constantly looking at each other's beard and hair; we were afraid that she would suddenly close the curtain and leave forever.

One day, after two months of standing on one corner and repeating everything we did, she seemed to realize that we were tired of it. She stood up suddenly, took the painting from the easel, and put another canvas in its place. This time we stood by the store and did things that would allow her to paint us from another angle. Once again, by repeating everything we did, we helped her to finish her work quickly and flawlessly.

We spent our days like that, and at night, when the bookstore had closed and she had stood up and drawn the curtain, we left together. We couldn't let each other go, as if we did not want to be alone or were afraid that something might suddenly happen, might have already happened, without one of us knowing. That's why we each took turns—no one knows how this system got started, since none of us had said a word—having everyone over to someone's house, where we'd sit and empty bottles. At first we only drank slowly—none of us wanted to drink more than the others. Everyone wanted to stay clear-headed so he could hear what the others said, so no spoken word would go unheard . . . But no one talked about anything besides paint, canvas, painting, Cezanne, and Van Gogh . . . We talked about things we had only recently understood; we spent a moment on the subject of Van Gogh's cut ear; we were sure that he'd had a pretty white earlobe, and that's why we cried sometimes. Late at night everyone would fall into a corner and listen to each other's loud drawn-out sighs for a long time. We knew that each of us, in a drunken world, awake or asleep, was reviewing his move-

ments of that day so he would be able to stand the same way
the next day, and not impede her work.

After a while we realized that sometimes between two
o'clock and a quarter to three she would go to the bookstore—that's why we were usually there by one . . . she would
come, nod her head, look at the books, and not buy anything.
We saw that she seemed to be watching us, as if she wanted
to examine us and see whether or not we were all there . . .
That's why, without a word being spoken, we were all there
by one o'clock. After a week of coming at one o'clock, we
saw her smile. She seemed to be pleased. We smiled too,
among ourselves, and stood and watched. We stood so that
she could see all of us, and each of us wished she could see
him better.

We saw her get out of a taxi a few times. A taxi or a small
pickup, we don't remember now exactly which it was, but
she had a load with her—an easel or a bed or something.
When she'd gotten out of the pickup, she started dragging her
load with difficulty. We were standing there watching, and
we saw the driver help her. Before we could move a muscle
or take a step, she had opened the little door to let the driver
in so he could carry her things upstairs. We looked at each
other in disbelief, standing like statues. We saw that the
driver was young and swarthy, with a thick mustache. He
was putting his money into his pocket as he came out the
door. He shut the little gate behind him, and before we could
go talk to him, he had gotten into his car, put his foot on the
gas, and left. We realized that day that none of us knew how
to drive, and later no matter how long we looked for the swarthy driver in the city, we couldn't find him.

Once we even dragged ourselves to face the door that he
had opened. Small steps, gray or lead-blue, and dark. We
thought the lightbulb in the stairwell must have burned out,
but none of us knew anything about electricity. That day we
looked at the streetlights and thought about the people who
climb the poles to fix the cables.

We remember the date of her departure well. The day that
all of us suddenly grew old, and well . . . none of us had seen
her leave, but she had left, and probably in the dark of night.

She hadn't left on Friday, because on Fridays we used to pass that street, sometimes on foot, sometimes in a taxi . . . Though no one was there, the curtain was closed, and we didn't even see any calves, we went there.

When she left, the common need to either forget her or see her again brought us close. We talked together, this time about her, and in a loud voice. We didn't know how, but we all realized that she had loved somebody once, or two people had loved her at the same time. They had gotten themselves killed in a fight over her, or maybe one had killed the other, and that other one left alive had been sentenced to death in a court. Her house overlooked the execution square, and every day she rose with the dawn to sketch the sunrise. She saw the sleepy soldiers who were taking that other one to his execution that other one walking in front of the soldiers, taking deep breaths . . . maybe because of her scent, which was still in the air. Maybe that other one knew she got up early every morning to sketch the sunrise, and knew how often she stayed awake at her window until morning. That is how we suddenly understood that she had dressed in black ever since, and mournfully devoted herself to painting, intending to have exhibitions in various cities. And that's why we listened, and still listen, to all the news of the arts, to see in which city a woman wearing black is having an exhibition.

In the first months we would all go to the bus terminal to ask if a woman artist in black was among the passengers. But now we think that we should take turns; one of us should go to the bus terminal every day, watch the passengers get off the bus, and tell the others later whether she came or not. It's not a difficult job. What we suffer, awake and asleep, is more difficult . . . Sometimes without letting on to each other, we wish we could sleep in our sleep, and not think of her. But we are always awake when we sleep, and if we sleep in that wakefulness, we dream we are awake; that is why it is getting harder, every day harder. If she had gone upstairs and closed the door and even the curtain, if she had covered all the windows, we wouldn't have gotten like this. Because we know that if our minds become pure, she will come again some day and hang up her short curtain. And we will see those two calves again, and a hand reaching under the table for a pencil, a brush . . . that has fallen, and then we will feel the tingling shoot through our calves again.

Every day that passes, even this instant, becomes the past, and no one can change the past. I mean, no one can change this instant, today, tomorrow, or the days to come. We know that fear, the fear we always carry with us, will not let us go, is addicted to us, is afraid to leave. As if it would have no other place in which to stay alive, to breathe, were it to leave . . . if it should leave . . . That is why we are always afraid; we are afraid of the future that is also the past. We are afraid that she will come again and think that we have forgotten her . . .

19 DECEMBER 1990
TEHRAN
TRANSLATED BY DYLAN OEHLER-STRICKLIN

Jeyran

To Khoda'i, the writer of the original Jeyran story . . .

As was her usual habit, she bent backward so that her hair fell loose onto the man's head and face, but the man didn't grab her hair, as was his usual habit, and didn't pull her head down to his chest as he always did and he didn't kiss her mouth and there was no shot of booze to pour on the corner of her lips and she did not drop down next to him, loop her two hands around his neck, and pull his head down and kiss the wrinkle in the corner of his eyes. She no longer knew him. He was frowning; she didn't recognize his frown.

She twirled, her pleated skirt puffed up. Her legs balanced again and she calmly retreated. The flute player changed the tone of his flute, the storm and the whirlwind that were blazing, or the fire, the fire of a thousand lit candles that flared up and burned everything, and the sound, the sound of columns falling, the columns that were collapsing on top of one another. The structure of a house was crumbling. The structure of a home, if it existed . . .

Circling the gathering, on top of the covered pool canopied by an old walnut tree, and next to each walnut and between the leaves and branches, lights: blue, red, green. And the light was woven into the fibers of her dress and the skin of her body and even her eyelids and her throat, which was swollen, and her cheeks, still burning from the flames of the candles.

She was drunk, Jeyran, dead drunk. And the sound was not putting out the flames of the candles. The tall flames of the candles.

"Think about yourself, think about your tomorrow."

The man had said it the last time when he was leaving, and

she, Jeyran, had swallowed her grief and said, . . . Let it go already . . . and the man had laughed like all the others who had laughed and like all the others who had said it the last time, and this time, it was the flames of the candle, a candle on the palm of her hands, until morning, until dawn, hands scorched with candles, and heart and eyes, her whole body.

She twirled on top of the pool. The plank was very sturdy this time, not like four years ago when the stamp of a foot had caved it in and the man who was very tall and broad-shouldered with a thick, black mustache and two drunk eyes had pulled her out of the pool and with one arm around her shoulder had taken her out of the gathering and had softly said, "You're drunk, Jeyran . . ."

She was drunk and dancing. Among the flames, not like a half-burned log that smoked and did not burn. She burned. Everything, all of the days and moments, all around her, eyes eager for the movement of her legs and chest, and the women who were staring so that when alone and in private, shaking their heads and moving their shoulders in front of their real men, and even this, they could take even this one short moment from her, envious and frightened eyes that wanted to easily drive her image, her transitory, disheveled image, into space, so that nothing remained for her . . . nothing.

The walls of the vast courtyard were moving toward her. The world was closing in on her, closer, and the raucous sound and the ululating were resonating in her ear. A sharp pain ran through Jeyran's legs, her ankle had swollen, and she was shaking her complaining, pleading hands toward the sky, a sky that was full of stars. And she was speaking with the stars, the distant stars.

"So where is it? Where is it? You wanted me to be this."

She had left for Qasroddasht Street late at night, when all of the women who have a hearth and home do not come out anymore, and she had left with a black chador and the packages of candles. She had lit them. And she had sat until morning crying, waiting for Samad, who had not shown up, to return; and the man had come, but one day at sunset, and he was not himself anymore, a vast, unconfined silence, and Jeyran had moaned to the stars . . . Where is it? Where is it? It was you who wanted me to be this . . .

She jumped down from the top of the pool as if her foot had hit the edge of something, maybe a carpet, and a hand from the circle of men caught her in the air and a voice said: Just say the word, Jeyran, I'm at your service . . .

And four years ago when she came with the musicians, wearing a flowered chador with a bundle of clothes in her hands and the same tall man with broad shoulders and a black mustache, which he did not have tonight, and two drunken eyes, which were not there tonight, had grabbed her flowered chador:

"Just say the word, Jeyran."

Many had said it and she had gone and not gone and then, when he took her to the room, soaking wet, the same two drunken eyes said:

"Jeyran, you've become like a fish . . ."

And Jeyran, not as drunk as tonight, had gently leaned her head forward and said in the man's ear: slippery . . . and the man had looked around so no one would see, he had stretched out his hands and she glided out from the circle of his arms and the soft flesh of her thigh had remained between the man's two fingers and she had said: Ouch!

The burning sting in her thigh and a hand that had come out from the circle of men, she frowned and twirled around . . . in honor of the bride and groom . . . her body, her soul, whipped, a scorched body, burned by the flame of the candles . . . until the light of dawn, her eyes and the flames of the candles on the palms of her hands, until morning. And each moment the whip of jeering and ululating on her soul, her legs, and he who had been standing next to the bride with his right hand on his chest bowing, laughing, and had said: See you, Jeyran.

He had said it and had laughed behind his black mustache.

"At your wedding."

"In twenty years, you rascal?"

With the tip of her toes and the playful drumlike sound, she slid like a rabbit on the carpet. She liked to see his hands. The hand that later on had stroked her head, had played with her hair.

"Here, put your hand on my forehead."

He was playing with her hair and Jeyran heard the sound of

a small creek passing on a plain, a green plain, and she had remained awake with two long candles on the palms of her hands so that the brook would sing and remain, forever.

She had reached the man. Near him and with one more leg movement, she could get his hand, a man who, it seemed, did not know her. He had neither drunken nor kind eyes and above his lip was white, very white, and he wasn't looking and was talking with a girl who was gently pushing back a lock of her hair under the bridal veil, and the girl and that dress, the long white dress.

She went every now and then to that square, hiding from familiar people, looking through the shop window and staring at the long dresses, white with lace around the sleeves and a puffy skirt and the silver sequins on them. And how soon the dresses were gone from the window and she, Jeyran, often and every night danced for this one and that. And this one, she had looked at it a lot and knew its price, cheap . . . it was the money she could get from one night of dancing without any problem, from just twirling enthusiastically, 3,000— only 3,000 tomans, if the man wanted and the stars, if those distant stars wanted and the man who said at sunset that day . . . everything is expensive.

And Jeyran took him. She could wear it only once, right there, in the store, standing next to him, next to the man, in front of the mirror, only once. The salesman laughed. He had seen her before, but didn't know her, Jeyran. If he had understood he wouldn't have laughed . . . Ma'am, may I offer you my congratulations? . . . And Jeyran got the dress from the salesman. Her hand was shaking. A sharp pain ran through her leg and the man looked at her . . . how beautiful . . . it fit her and the salesman's lips quivered . . . aren't you going to try it on for alteration, ma'am? . . .

The man had laughed hard and Jeyran only paid for the dress and she had seen the look on the salesman's face, dejected, disappointed . . .

With a rapid movement, she bent over and her hair fell loose, a curtain between her and the others. She moved her shoulders smoothly and stayed still so she could hold back her tears . . . once, even once, between the white voile.

She felt a pain ricochet in her ankle. Her knees trembled. She sat down. She bent over. Her hands parallel to the ground, with a slight movement of her shoulders, she swallowed her tears.

"It's like small ocean waves . . . I have been to the north."

"The Caspian Sea isn't a real sea."

And the man was grabbing her earlobe:

"Where are you from, where?"

She had said: "Ask me where I have been and what I have been doing."

"What business is it of mine, woman? So, you earn a living."

"What living!"

"Come with me, anywhere, everywhere. When you're not here, I'm like a garden without a wall."

And the man was watching: "If it's not a familiar place."

And everything she owned was in the man's account. She was fond of saying: Money for expenses! And the man, like every other man in the world, took some money out of his pocket and threw it on her lap, and the man simply said: "So, what does it have to do with me?"

And Jeyran, choked with tears, would close the man's lips with her index finger, lie down with her head on his knee, and take a spoonful of yogurt so the man, just like a child, brought his head down, opened his mouth, and said: "I am dead drunk . . ."

When he was dead drunk, he wouldn't pay attention to his surroundings and it was Jeyran, his own Jeyran, who said, "I'm yours, I'm your slave-maid, Samad." And the man, holding his mouth with his hand, slowly and solemnly said, "No, don't say slave, don't say it," and Jeyran would hear the sound of his weeping, "You're nice, so nice, if only you weren't, you weren't . . ."

And so that Jeyran wouldn't, wouldn't be anymore, with packages of candles she would go at midnight and stay there until morning, standing against the wind so that the flames wouldn't blow out . . . *do something if you don't want me to be . . .*

And now he was sober next to the girl, sometimes fixing his collar and sneaking a peek, as if Jeyran wasn't there, wasn't there at all, and when she had come early in the night, she hadn't seen him. She had looked around here and there was a woman's voice saying: "They haven't come from the beauty shop yet . . ."

"You're nice, so nice . . . what do you want me to buy for you, Jeyran?"

"Two loaves of bread. Two fresh, hot loaves of *barbari* bread."

She liked the man to come from work tired with two loaves of barbari bread, to sit on the windowsill waiting for him and then pour water on his hands and hand him the towel, a towel that smelled like rosewater. The man only came in the evenings or on Fridays to have a drink.

The flute had a peaceful tone. She stood up on her toes. She turned and stood in front of the man. With her fingertips she caught both sides of her dress, moved her feet gently. The man's frown and the pain that she felt in her ankle had reached her knee. The girl put her head next to the man's ear as if saying something, as if signaling to him, and the man shrugged his shoulder and snickered. She felt the pain at the top of her thigh, was on the verge of tears when very slowly, the tone of the reed flute pulled her out of the circle of the gathering.

In that same room one day, she had changed her wet dress. She came face to face with a woman whom her distracted mind recognized. It was Samad's sister-in-law . . . she stood motionless! And this child who had grabbed her skirt . . . Mama . . . and the time had passed so easily, so hard. The woman was happy. Her cheeks had flushed with joy . . . Mama . . . and Jeyran was disgusted with herself and alienated by everything, with whatever reeked of existence. She swallowed her sorrow.

"I want to change my costume."

She closed the door, staring at the knob as though it might move. It didn't move, she knew. She turned around and saw her maroon-colored dress . . . Mama . . . Mama . . . she hid her face between the puffs of her dress and cried bitterly.

"You have to understand my situation, Jeyran."

She understood, she was Jeyran; the man was sober and she, drunk out of her mind. And Jeyran, who was Jeyran, had nothing to say. What could she say? Who would believe her? She was only Jeyran, wasn't she? And it had been six months since she had had a drink. And every night at midnight, she went to the street with the lit candles or stayed in the house. Two tall, lit candles, burning until morning in the palms of her hands, scorching . . .

"Let's drink to your wedding."

And the man didn't. "And it's a little late, but there are no rumors about her, not a word."

Jeyran quietly would raise her glass, every moment her throat burned, her hands and her whole body scorched.

"You aren't upset?"

No! She said it firmly, because it was Jeyran and many had said, At your service, Jeyran, and she had or had not gone and this one . . . the wind . . . the wind . . . had surely blown out all the candles.

"It was very hard for me to say it. I wanted to leave it as it is and flee, but I told myself, You might go crazy, come home . . . thank God. A person is at ease with folks like you, now if it were a girl . . ."

She was cold . . . The lifeless, withering flames gave no warmth, and because of what the man had said, she slipped into his arms, a warm and uncertain place. She put her cold, frozen arms around the man's neck: "Let go, now." The man had said: "You should think about yourself, too, find somebody to take you away from all this."

Her body, scorched. Her heart. The flames of the candles, the way she had looked at them, burning drop by drop, and had shielded them from the gusts of wind, and now they were burning and melting in the hollow of her heart and, ah. If she sighed, it would blow them out . . . she wouldn't sigh. Jeyran was drunk, drunk out of her mind. The doorknob was moving. In disbelief, she searched with hope and fear. It was a young man who had a kind, coy smile on his lips. The first smile.

"They're waiting for you, Miss Jeyran!"

The young man looked around, closed the door, and left. Jeyran wore her maroon dress, the same maroon dress the man had once liked. She didn't understand who handed her the microphone and who sang with her sorrowful voice: "May the world never be without the sound of the lover's wailing."

When her voice choked, she threw the microphone. She wanted to put out the flames, if only they could be put out with the tapping of her foot. She screamed: Southern port music. The sound of the reed flute grew louder and the beat of her feet was in step with the salty smell of the sea that poured onto the courtyard. It was stormy and an ownerless and anchorless ship was going up and down on high waves . . . her head down, she moved her shoulders and arms like waves in a storm, and like a whirlwind she twisted around herself and screamed out the words of the song: "Captain, come and cast a glance at the waves of the sea."

With the firm, strong movement of her feet, she came forward. She got closer and she saw she could count the wrinkles at the corner of the man's eyes and she could see the curve of his waist and his thighs, the same place she used to hide her hand like a scared seagull in a storm. A place where she could hide her face, in its depths . . . She got a drink from a young hand and a soft chorus of "cheers" rose from the gathering, and it seemed she had never kissed the man. She had never seen his hand and never smelled the corners of his eyes and he was going forever. He was going far, far away. He was going with the whirlwind that was blowing out the thousands of candle flames, he was going . . .

She couldn't stand anymore. Looking and waiting, she came closer and bent over toward the man. The man pulled back and looked at her angrily. And Jeyran, between fear and trembling feet, reached for the bride's shoulders, bent toward the girl, and kissed her oily cheeks. And the man, terrified, pushed Jeyran away with the palm of his hand. Jeyran staggered back . . . a sea wave slowly tumbling over itself. When it was over, she put on her flowered chador and put the bundle of clothes under her arm. Staggering, she went toward the door. The young man reached forward to hold her arm. She pushed him back with her elbow. The man was standing next to the door and was shaking hands with the flute player. When Jeyran got there, he put his right hand on his chest, bowed slightly, and cleared his throat but said nothing. He took an envelope out of his pocket. Jeyran leaned against the wall and took the envelope. Three new bills . . . with two fingers she carefully held the bills away from herself. The man, sneaking a look, took several steps forward and saw her pale face. A bitter smile had settled on Jeyran's lips. She put the bills into the man's pocket and with a raspy, drunken voice said:

"Where there has been love, payment is unnecessary . . . unnecessary."

MAY—JUNE 1990
SHIRAZ
TRANSLATED BY PERSIS KARIM

Haros

To Janet Lazarian

Hasmik was tall. She had a round face and eyes that always had two teardrops rolling around in them. When you looked at her you would get distracted and think to yourself that any moment now those two tears would slide down her cheeks and reach the wrung-out creases around her lips. Sorrowful, colorless lips that quivered for no reason and made one think she was about to speak or scream. A scream was frozen right there on her lips.

The skiers were scattered all over the slope. Hasmik, with large dark glasses, a scarf that she had pulled up over her nose, and a woolen cap that covered her cheeks, could easily think . . . and allow those two captive tears to slip without any fear or apprehension and slide down her cheeks.

Now no one could see her face and say: So much patience at this age? Patience was the only thing she no longer had. That enormous, wide-open house with all those pictures framed on its walls, that house in which for so long no sound had been heard but the ringing of the telephone. The sound of the ringing of the telephone and the sound of her cries directed at the walls, the cold and frowning walls. That house had left her no patience. When the memories would suddenly attack and the pain would twist in her throat and Hasmik would punch the walls that moment by moment were closing in and before she would be crushed by the pressure of the walls and the distant, long rings of the telephone, she would leave the house. She would either spin around and

Note: Haros means "hero" in Armenian.

around herself in that huge yard and, with an eye on the neighbors' windows, pull her scarf over her forehead, or she would go into the empty pool, draw the Persian letter for *T*, pick up the paintbox and busy herself until a head would emerge from the windows and she would hear . . . really, what patience . . . then she would squeeze her throat with her hand and scream.

And now she had come here, in the frozen air, amid the skiers who were certainly young. She was careful with the small and large turns, and would struggle to round the fast turns and become so tired that during the nighttime, when she would lay her head on the pillow, she would not toss and turn until the late hours.

She watched. The skiers occasionally stood next to one another and talked. Wherever several skiers gathered, you could say without seeing their faces that they were all young. Youthful and young in years. Loneliness and youth do not go together. You cannot imprison any youth in the frame of a house, you cannot give him the promise of better days, the youth will not stay. Even if you bring him here, in the stubborn, heedless white of the snow and the wind and cold that is always here. Then he will scream and yell at you:

"But we can't, Mama . . ."

She still couldn't believe it, Christmas would come and she would have to go sit in that house with a pine tree and listen to the ringing of the telephone without hearing the voice of Haros: "Mama . . . Ali . . ."

Words that he would remember exactly on holidays to make everything bitter in Hasmik's mouth and in his own. Hasmik no longer exerted any effort to weave words and change his mind—something that she had managed to do for seven years. She thought that she had been able to distance him from what was in his mind . . . and that was Ali and the date palms and the house in that town that no longer was.

It had started from that time, from that moment when they were escaping. Haros was crying and Ali was there, too, with big hazel eyes and curly hair . . . the little boy didn't want to cry, but there were tears in his eyes and he wanted to stay there . . . he was no more than thirteen. His hand was on Haros' shoulder, he said nothing, it seemed as if he just swallowed, something moved up and down in his throat. There was the distant sound of artillery and Haros, who was pounding on Hasmik's chest with his fists, didn't want to go with them, with Helen, his sister, and Hasmik, who was barefoot and was pulling him toward a truck. When they boarded, she held him tight so that he would not throw himself off in the direction of the little boy who was crying. Hasmik held Haros' face in both hands so he would not turn and see the tears that were sliding down the boy's black cheeks.

When they came to Tehran, Haros was always a southerner and with the southerners, and maybe they filled in the story of the little boy in his mind. The little boy who gets hit in the belly by a ricocheting bullet and who, holding on with a wounded right arm, doubled over in pain, goes on and reaches the barbed wire fence and opens his arms in the air and throws himself on the fence so others can pass over him.

Haros would open his arms like a bird, and would throw himself and scream, and Hasmik would listen patiently. She thought that it would end one day when he got older, but Haros' glance changed from year to year, from a look of pleading, the pleading of a child who wants to get his mother's permission to do something, something beyond his years, it changed and became a hostile and spiteful glance—eyes that stared as if at a prison guard and would not stop. He would speak so that perhaps the memories would come back to life in Hasmik's mind, too. He would speak to soften Mama's heart, and it had been years since Hasmik had heard the sound of the breaking of her heart, and she could no longer pick up the broken fragments. The sound of the cannons and mortar shells wouldn't let her, the sound of the people who would leave their windows open and with puzzled black eyes would say . . . Hello, madame . . . what patience, madame.

They were both children. Ali a year older. When he was seven he came to their house for the first time. He was wearing baggy pants that he was always pulling up. He took off his tennis shoes right there by the door and, with hands on his knees, sat politely in a corner. When everyone sat around and Helen spoke to him he stared in wonder at them and said with surprise, "Then why don't you talk like foreigners?"

Haros punched the little boy in the arm and said, "Why

should we talk like foreigners? We aren't foreigners." The
boy had looked at all of them again, at Helen, at Hasmik,
at Haros. He had waved his hand in the air in confusion
and said, "But everyone thinks you're foreigners." Helen had
covered her mouth with her hand. Haros had laughed out
loud . . . "Foreigners . . . Oh! Foreigners." The boy seemed to
be reassured. He stretched out his legs and later they even
wrestled. From the kitchen, Helen and Hasmik could hear
the sound of their laughter . . .

Those days Helen still felt all right. She wasn't afraid of
anything and would not always whisper in Hasmik's ear:
"Mama, all the villages of Urmia have been deserted . . .
Mama, don't say homeland so much . . ."

Hasmik had known for a long time that a hot salt-en-
crusted earth loves tall date palms. From the time when the
artillery would fire, "Madame . . . Madame," and the fragments of her heart would become smaller. The artillery had
always been there, and was now much more evident, and
continuous, much more than before.

Now Helen knew, too, and if sometimes a smile would
settle on Hasmik's lips it was because she understood that
Helen knew, too. When the phone would ring and from the
other side of the world a hoarse and grief-stricken voice
would try to be cheerful and strong and say, "Where did you
go, Mama? Where did you go today? When will you go south,
Mama? What's happening, Mama?"

How could Helen live with that man whom Hasmik still
did not recognize after four years when she looked at his pictures? She always thought that this time when her eye fell on
the picture, she would see that boy by Helen, with his bril-
liant hazel eyes and the tear that had slid down his cheeks
that last time. But there was always someone else next to
Helen. A strange and unfamiliar man. And when Haros was
there he knew too why Helen said imploringly, "I didn't want
it; I went to the hospital and got rid of it . . . then everything
would have been complicated." And Hasmik knew that Helen had once loved children.

The slope was closing. Hasmik didn't want to return home
before it was dark. The empty house and the pictures that
stared at her and the Karun River that in various photographs

seemed always to be overflowing. She heaved a sigh and started out sluggishly. She had to catch the minibus. The minibus stopped every few feet and she could reach home at a time when there was no traffic in the street by their house and no one could see from behind a window into the darkness of the street and shoot.

She sat hunched over. The bus would stop every now and then, the tired skiers would get off; she was the last to get off at Ekhtiyariyyeh Square. It was still light, the glances that turned toward her and the bullets that were fired . . . Madame . . . Madame.

She set off on foot. She turned left. The falling of the snow had not been able to tear the pictures, the pictures on the wall and the various anniversaries. The large hazel eyes of the photographs weakened her steps. She smiled bitterly, the little boy in the picture had grown taller, had gotten older, and then it was finished . . . and what things remained to torture a person, what memories and glances . . .

Hasmik was still standing there staring at the hazel eyes of the photograph, passersby looked at the ski poles of the tired skier and walked on, hunched over in the cold.

Quite late, she became conscious of the heavy stares of the passersby. An old man, his profile turned toward her, had not seen the gutter and had slipped and fallen.

She rubbed her eyes, pulled the scarf up over her nose, now nobody saw her face, a face reddened from crying and cheeks full of wrinkles.

A voice said: Madame . . . Madame. Hasmik looked. The felled pines by the side of the street and Christmas coming and everything just as it was except for that voice she no longer heard, that tired and obstinate voice:

"You said the same thing last year, too, you say the same thing every year . . . wait 'till you grow up, wait 'till you grow up."

And Hasmik had tried for seven years to put stories together to tell Haros, Haros who had stranger stories that he would remember on holiday evenings when he would decorate the pine tree. Harry was now grown up and you couldn't cheer him up with a Christmas present.

"Mama, do you remember that New Year's Eve . . ."

That night Ali had stayed. Hasmik had put things under the pine tree for both of them, the little boy, who didn't want to sleep without seeing Santa Claus, had fallen asleep with his head on Helen's knee.

It was two o'clock in the afternoon when the radio announced the news, first in summary and then fully. Hasmik hugged Harry, Haros, who was now grown up, and yelled: "You see . . . you see, if you had gone?"

But two days later she didn't dare kiss him, a man who was bent over tying his shoelaces. And they had reached Hamidiyyeh Garrison. Haros said:

"Mama . . . this radio is lying . . . they've taken the city again."

It was as if she'd never heard his voice like this. A manly, husky voice. Because she had so much wanted always to fool that little boy, a little boy who had wanted to pursue his own fate, and she had not let him until that day when she suddenly heard his voice, after seven years, she heard the voice of a man whom she could no longer entertain with any story.

She turned into an alley, she leaned against a wall and closed her eyes. Harry had said that Ali is buried in a cemetery in the city in a place where, if you sit and close your eyes, the wind blows among the flags and anyone can hear the sound of their screaming.

And Hasmik didn't know where she should hear the sound of Harry's screams, where she should sit and close her eyes to hear Harry's screams, "Mama, this radio is lying . . . it's lying . . ."

Tired and heavy-hearted, she started out. It was still not completely dark and she no longer had the strength to walk. She was going home to a cold and empty house, a cold that she feared and always wished she could forget, but couldn't.

She looked, drew a breath in relief. There was no one in the street, the doors and windows were closed, and muted light shone from behind lace curtains. She stepped slowly and sluggishly, with the ski boots that she had dragged with her and now felt heavy.

She had reached the door, the big white door. Her hand trembled, she was searching in her pocket and could not find the key. It was always like this when she reached home, she had to search, in her pocket or her purse, the key would suddenly get lost. She turned at a sound. The window of the neighbor across the street had opened, the neighbor's wife laughed in the window frame:

"You must be tired, madame. Have you just come back from skiing?"

She became confused, she cringed in mute agitation, she smiled bitterly, she searched her mind for the words that had suddenly fled.

"Good for you, madame . . . you are different from us!"

She stood in the yard by a garden that had frozen under the snow. The sound of bullets spun in her ears:

Good for you, madame . . . you are different from us.

DECEMBER 1988
TEHRAN
TRANSLATED BY ATOOSA KOUROSH

Play

A pesky wind, obstinate and persistent, twisted around the bare branches of the tree until it separated the last leaf from it. It was the month of Azar, the last month of autumn. Maryam watched from behind the railing. The girl was still sitting on the stairs of the Literature Building. The autumn wind was lifting the fallen leaves into the air.

Bored, Maryam stood up. She picked up her bag full of papers and books. She went under the tree, reached out, caught a dried leaf, clenched her fist, and listened to the crisp, crumbling sound of the leaf. She laughed. She started to walk alongside the railing of the College of Literature. She heard the shrill ringing of the bell; adrenaline rushed through her. She walked into the open area. Hesitant and uncertain, the girl got up from the stairs. Her eyes were red and puffy. Maryam climbed the stairs. Old theater posters on the walls. Her glance slid over the pictures and saw the man at the end of the corridor coming with a briefcase in his hand. He was wearing a blue checkered shirt. His hair hung down to his shoulders. He was walking, oblivious to the girl who had just come up to him. The girl was waving her hands. She was wiping her cheeks and was pulled toward the man.

She turned toward the old poster, it was from three months ago . . . she read the names . . . the director and actors . . . the actress . . . she reached into her bag anxiously. She pulled out a book from between the other books and papers and shook her head. She zipped her bag shut and turned back toward the corridor.

The corridor of the college was still crowded. The man was making his way through the crowd. The girl was following close behind. She held a hand over her mouth. Her shoulders were trembling.

When the man reached her, he smiled. He took a deep breath and said:

"I have kept you waiting . . ."

When they left the Literature Building they saw the girl leaning against the wall and holding her face in both hands. As always, the man turned to the right toward Hafeziyyeh. He was frowning. He seemed to be tired.

"She can't act . . . I have told her a hundred times . . ."

"She had a part in the last play . . ."

"Yes, but looks alone won't do. For this part, I need a voice, a voice that will project . . ."

She pulled herself up and swallowed her smile. She unzipped her bag and pulled out the book.

"I have memorized all the dialogues."

"Leave it for later . . . when we are sitting down."

They reached the door of Hafeziyyeh. The man stroked his blond beard; he stood behind the garden fence, the wind scattered the remaining petals.

"Such weather! So dusty . . ."

The man was tired. He spoke in chopped and heavy phrases. He was not his usual self: He was not looking at her.

"My house is close by and there is hot tea, too; we can do a couple of scenes there . . ."

2

She said:

"Should we talk about the play?"

The man rolled over and said in a tired voice:

"Now? Leave it for later."

There wasn't a sound coming from the street. The raindrops pelted against the window panes. Maryam looked at the golden, sweat-drenched hair that had fallen on his forehead and at his white body that lay stretched out beside her.

The man's eyes were closed. Maryam stroked his forehead and said:

"Do you think I can?"

The man remained as he was, and with his eyes closed said:

"Can what?"

"That I can get the part of Antigone."

The man mumbled in a sleepy voice:

"Yeah, sure . . . you just . . ."

He began to snore. Maryam looked at him expectantly. The man's snores became more rhythmic. Maryam said softly:

"Are you asleep?"

She pulled the sheet over his naked body, which now embarrassed her. She turned her face away. The room was small and gray. Books were scattered here and there on the floor of the room. A photograph of a bespectacled old man with a goatee on the wall. Maryam distanced herself from the man. She picked up a book and opened it: "I love you as much as all the women I do not know, Your belly . . . "[1]

Bored, she shut the book. She stretched out on her stomach and rested her chin on her hands. Outside the window the sky was dark. It was drizzling. She looked at the man gloomily. With two long, slender fingers, she lifted the man's eyelids and saw his cold, blue irises. The man did not move. Maryam withdrew her hand. She looked at the bespectacled man and the books again. Bored, she sat up and said loudly: Well . . .

And joyfully she stared at the wall. An ant was climbing up the wall. With her finger she blocked the ant's path.

"How are you? Where are you going? Come, let's talk. No, don't run away; I'm not going to hurt you; we will only talk. Have you ever been to the theater? You haven't? Maybe you've crawled in between the seats. If you haven't been, you have to know that I . . . act in plays. This man asleep here is a director . . . Where are you going? Do you want me to show you the book . . . do you want me to read for you . . . listen . . . In my mourning there shall rise neither a sigh to the sky, nor shall a tear drop on the ground. Hey, wait; I swear I won't hurt

1. From Octavio Paz's long poem "Sunstone."

you. Yes, now . . . today we have become friends . . . but we should not take these things seriously . . . You know, he says that I can act. He said it himself . . . What do you say? Don't go . . . you are such a character. Are you scared of the sound of his snoring—of his snoring? Wait . . . wait, let me show you the book . . ."

The ant was escaping . . . rain kept falling and the man snored on.

SEPTEMBER 1983

TEHRAN

TRANSLATED BY REZA SHIRAZI

Another Version

There are various accounts about her, born at four o'clock in the morning in a small village by the sea. These stories are still passed around, from one to another, and you can check with anyone as to whether they are true or false, except for her; she died at four o'clock in the morning in a crowded, overpopulated city.

They say she was absolutely unconscious when she was born. Everyone knows this, the woman in labor who is now old and sits in the corner, the wet nurse who at four in the morning that day was sleepily present beside the woman in labor, and the others who had been awakened suddenly from their sleep by the screams of the woman giving birth.

Everyone who was so suddenly awakened that bothersome morning describes the moments before the birth like this: "A male lion was born and its roars filled the village sky."

Those optimists who are old now and on their way out have no clear answer to the question of why a newborn would be born unconscious, by the seaside, no less. Nevertheless, this writer guesses otherwise and wishes that life had not placed her in a distant city that morning at four o'clock, or at least that her sleep would not have been so deep that she wasn't awakened by the screams of the woman in labor.

If—and this is just a suppressed wish—she had been there, she would have seen the behavior and actions of the people around, and she would have heard what they said, and she would have been able to say with a clear conscience that the newborn was unconscious from the start or was born this way or that way or had seen someone or heard someone that caused her to become unconscious. With all this, this writer, who considers herself to be reasonably perceptive and is interested in only two things—planting beets and finding out about other people's lives—has not for a moment stopped trying and has worked hard listening to different people's versions, which are not very different from each other, and has reached certain conclusions; for instance, she now knows that in that situation, everyone had been yawning, and everyone stood back from the woman in labor out of fear and dread. The other thing she knows is that the wet nurse had heard the lion's roars in her sweet morning sleep and her whole body shook, and a hen crowed a cock-a-doodle-doo in place of a lazy rooster that had not had the patience to carry out its morning duties. The morning sky had been colorful, and splotches of red clouds rose in the sky over the village with no wind to move them. (Let it be noted that the newborn's father later considered those splotches a sign of the bloodshed that the newborn would start in the world.) And a thousand other things that there is no particular use in repeating.

But the situation was different for the newborn's father. Apparently he was sitting in a corner fearlessly counting his regrets on his fingers. The wet nurse, who was also watching the father of the newborn, could also easily count regrets. The newborn's father, about whom this writer later reached the conclusion that he was born to be regretful, in that murderously long morning wait, was sighing; he was shaking his head and sometimes laughing to himself—the wet nurse, who also smokes a water pipe, told this writer: "When the newborn came into the world and everything became clear, the man banged his head hard against the wall and screamed three times."

The writer presumes that the newborn child probably became completely unconscious with one of these screams, because that newborn child who had not been born yet could eavesdrop and would tremble with fear upon hearing the impossible dreams of its father who was laughing. This version, which is based on assumptions and suppositions only, is supported by the accounts of the people who later came in contact with the newborn (who was grown up by then) in different cities. All of those people, young and old, agree that the newborn sighed sometimes and spoke in a strange, drawn-out voice within the very first seconds of birth . . . there are other versions as well. One of these was that during the nine months and nine days of its existence the newborn had heard talk that was often about itself and did not want to come out; and when it did come and heard the screams of its father, it did not know where to go. They say that in those very first moments it went back toward its mother's legs again, but the mother, who had covered her eyes with her hands, pushed it away with her sore knee. Some are convinced that from that moment the newborn pretended to be completely unconscious (these people think that the newborn is excessively clever).

With all the rumors, it is obvious that all unconscious people continue their natural growth in a state of absolute unconsciousness. Essentially, when you are a newborn, no one pays much attention to these things; even if they do, they do not show it; or perhaps, according to the related versions, the inhabitants of that distant village had forgotten what a healthy newborn looks like.

Anyhow, the newborn was growing bigger. It drank milk with half-open eyelids; it cried with half-closed eyes; and sometimes it would breathe . . . They say that the mother, who was nursing her first newborn, would sometimes call those around her in amazement and point at the newborn's chest, which rose and fell slowly, saying with a tired and hoarse voice: "Ooh, it's dying, do you see?" And the wet nurse who was responsible for its condition, shaking her head, would say: "How long this will go on, God only knows . . ."

And the newborn, like all ordinary people whose chests do not have the slightest movement and do not even rise and fall, played and was pretty good at it. But sometimes it would stagger and lean to the left or right like a person who had been hit on the head but nonetheless had to get somewhere.

The newborn went to school later on—during this period the mother, in the hope of hearing the roar of the lion, gave birth to five or six babies, and the father, as usual, was counting his regrets, which kept increasing day by day—during this period the newborn learned many things. Especially from the comings and goings of the people who lived in the half-tones of its semi-closed eyelids. It had learned to walk straight and even swing its book satchel back and forth, and sometimes it would burst into song, but its voice was always strained and odd.

The newborn went to high school from grade school and from there, without even going home (now, they lived in a small town, probably like the port of Bushehr), went to the university. In college, two simple events happened to her. One was that she completely forgot her family—a part of the gray matter of her brain, the part related to her family, especially her father and her sisters, was damaged mysteriously— and in addition to this, the manner in which she walked changed. She was bent into herself, and all through her life she would walk hunched over.

People, all those who were always waiting to fabricate a story about every little detail, would resort to all sorts of wild and strange guesses and suppositions. Various narrators have said that just a little before she forgot her family, she had come to believe in some kind of motion, a spiral motion for that matter. And the father, who did not want to have any more regrets than he already had at four o'clock in the morning one winter's day, panicked, came out of the house, and denied everything in a loud voice. We should put the burden of proof on those who tell these stories; this narrator does not have much confidence in this version. At this hour, the newborn was burning papers in the courtyard of their house, and the smell of the burned papers and the scorched hopes had so intensified in the city that many people began to sneeze in their sleep and even breathing became difficult for them.

But this writer, who in the first years of college had been her classmate, frankly declares that the newborn's bending into herself and walking in a curved fashion was not related to pain from appendicitis or any other disease. Not to mention that surviving documents in medical school proved everything clearly (upon many visits and extensive searches through the newborn's files). Even after all this, the writer still cannot say why the newborn in its youth walked in a bent and confused way and why it sometimes composed poetry. The writer is afraid to announce that a pain much worse and deadlier than the pain of appendicitis had twisted the stomach and intestines of the newborn . . . probably, as the meteorology student at the college used to say, the invisible wind and rains that cannot be seen by just any eyes and that prevent any sort of spiral movement thrust the dust and debris onto the face of the newborn and had forced her to twist into herself like a shrimp.

But everyone knows how meteorology students are. Those who, with strange predictions, sink many ships and run them amok, and what ships! And the writer herself, who later witnessed many things running amok, does not put much faith in this kind of scientific analysis, and, in this case, is of the same opinion as the newborn. The newborn, who was growing day by day, finally one day got so big that it cast a half-open, half-closed, fully amorous look at a pair of glasses (the writer surmises that she can unduly take advantage of the term "sleepy" instead of "amorous" such that no one is offended)—the beginning of a love, or to put it another way, falling into a complete coma—but this moment did not last long, and therefore as soon as the newborn could line up sentences to write a letter, it had found itself sitting at a wedding ceremony. And what a wedding spread!

Whether it is true or not is the responsibility of those who say it. The newborn, apparently after finishing the bachelor's degree, reached the doctoral stage. One cannot say this with assurance due to this writer's chronic and excessive interest in beets before her birth. That is why she left college after a while and went to live close to the sea to find a piece of land and get busy with planting. But, as she has also heard it, apparently the newborn had received a bachelor's degree, and also a master's. And later on when she died, her classmates were thinking with astonishment about the unwavering and repetitive question that she repeatedly asked her professors. And even this writer, in that calm and quiet atmosphere close to the land where the mysterious, underground noise of the beets, resembling a lullaby, put her to sleep time and time again, has frequently thought about the same persistent, odd, and strained question. The question that was full of struggle:

"H . . . o . . . w . . . a . . . r . . . e . . . you?"

Yes, the students still remember her ringing voice, which sometimes dragged on for two hours . . . For example, one day she wanted to say "life" and started with the *l* at eight o'clock in the morning and when school was over still sat on the chair facing the teacher's desk, searching for the *fe* in her mind.

Now, when people have a thousand things to do, who can sit around waiting for a woman who is over thirty to spell out words, or to strain from morning till night to say this worthless sentence: "Everything is spinning!"

They say that her marriage ceremony took place in Qir and Karzin around the time that the earthquake crumbled everything. Perhaps the newborn stood on ground that still trembled, with muddy, injured hands and dirt all over her hair and face. She sees glasses on a man's face, and right then she stops what she is doing and looks (a sleepy sideways look, not completely head on, a look that could cause gossip). As the newborn continues to look, she finds herself in a notary office, a notary office whose walls had crumbled. No one was there except a marriage clerk, all of whose bones had apparently been broken in the earthquake, but who stood obstinately on the pile of rubble so he could carry out the last of his earthly duties. At this moment, the clerk was writing something on the ground with his broken, pointing finger.

The newborn, who was thinking of escape, dragged herself behind the man to stand before the clerk. Words that came out of the newborn's mouth that day and the day after never went beyond: How . . . long . . . d . . . o . . . e . . . s . . . it . . . take? And when the clerk said five minutes, she—who in this interval had smirked and maybe even smiled—answered (in a voice so strained that the clerk had to wait two days for the sentence to finish): "Good. One can destroy the world in five minutes."

When the clerk performed the wedding ceremony, it was evening, two days later. Everyone was sleepy and she was concentrating all her attention on the sound of the jackals that were howling on the pile of rubble. So it is unknown whether she ever said "yes," taking into account the problem of the clerk's collapsing immediately on that pile of rubble and yielding his soul to the Creator. Nevertheless, as long as she was in Qir and Karzin, the world stayed in its place. One night, tired, she boarded a truck with the groom, who was also a student and muddy, and they came to Shiraz. The truck driver said of the situation: "God damn! Every minute of the hour she was messing with the guy's glasses. I saw her myself several times. When he dozed off, she tried to take off his glasses quietly, but he would jerk awake and push her hand away as though he were mad."

Later on, the groom said in astonishment to others (he declined to speak to this writer; he basically did not like planting beets):

"From the very beginning, she wanted to take my glasses so I couldn't see anything. On the road, I caught her two or three times in the act, but she wouldn't back off. When we got to the city, it was 2:30 in the morning and drizzling. The driver played a song with a beat to it, and my wife started moving around and nodding her head to the music. You should have seen her. The lyrics went like this: 'I'm tired, I'm tired, tired; I'm done in.' No matter how much I glared at her, she didn't get it. When we got off the truck on Zand Street, I threw her in a gutter . . . even then, when she got up, she reached out for my glasses."

Three months later the groom frees himself, and when the newborn comes to the college cafeteria, she stares at people as always, as though there had never been a wedding at all, or a marriage. Only in answering someone who asked how she was did she say in a strained, sleepy voice, "I . . . t . . . hit . . . m . . . e . . . in . . . the . . . head." Normally, when someone gets hit in the head, he doesn't die, and no one, no matter how many spiteful, ancient enemies there might be, can say that the newborn wasn't human. In short, people—all people—were caught up in their own affairs; the newborn grew up in the midst of busy people. She was so oblivious to her surroundings that suddenly she realized that years had gone by and she had no passport! This awareness came upon her with the arrival of another man; this time it was her father. The man who was still busy counting his regrets bellowed from his gut, "I am your father." A moment later, when the newborn believed him, he said a little softer, times have changed, and now no healthy person should be negligent of profit and loss. It was at that moment that the new-born understood, her sisters, her various sisters, had taken frequent trips abroad and had made up for their expenses.

This writer presumes that the newborn stood in line at the passport office so that she would be safe from her father's perpetual hounding. But different narrators say that the father had thought of the newborn because of the terror that had engulfed him in those days, and he had wanted to send the newborn, who was still hunched over while walking, beyond the borders. But this writer, who has been able to read the fragments of the newborn's disorganized notes (she paid black-market prices to obtain the notes from the newborn's sisters), has seen this sentence on a blank page among spiral lines that show the date of February 1984: Just give me the permit for your passport, just that.

Well! It is obvious from this sentence that she would leave the line and walk away, with a smile on her lips, and it is quite clear how the father was bellowing from his gut. But one cannot expect anything from our newborn, just as she had made fools of the people of a village years ago and instead of being born a male lion she came into this world unconscious, this time she laid it on the line, left her father, and went away and never again set eyes on anyone called "Father."

In another page of the newborn's diary, this writer has noticed a strange sentence that perhaps served as a model on a dark and stormy night. On a page dated 24 July 1988, this sentence has been written thirty-three times: "It is better to brush your teeth than to scream." This writer, who does not have much patience for reading old manuscripts, panicked and passed over this page in fear and has only reached the conclusion that the newborn lacked something, and this conclusion has not been arrived at easily, but only after a great deal of effort, and in writing the sentence "It is better to brush your teeth than to scream" three hundred and thirty times, she has stopped screaming.

Anyway, she lacked something. Something that was unknown to the end, even to herself, and even the people who would suddenly appear in front of her during the passport period and would ask, "Excuse me. Just now when you were coming from the intersection and were thinking, what were you thinking about?" could not figure out what she lacked.

Even on the day she died, she did not understand the meaning of dying. Only from the gathering of the crowd and some people's crying had she come to the conclusion that something had happened—still she did not understand why her sisters (strange and unfamiliar women who had appeared by her side as soon as she had died and were saying through their continuous wailing, Oh my dear sister . . .) had clung to all those papers and books, talking to each other like Siamese quadruplets, weighing the books.

When a thick book was torn to pieces in the hands of the mourning sisters, in that state of death and silence, the newborn had asked them to read the book in turn and not torment each other about a book that had not yet reached the black market. And it was at that moment that a smile had appeared on the lips of the four sisters.

Anyway, curse these cursed smiles that are on many people's lips, many whose sisters have not yet died. But different narrators agree wholeheartedly on one point: The ceremonies were conducted successfully.

But this writer does not give much credence to this version. It is true that the mournful sisters wanted everything to go well, but the earrings that were shining from under black veils bothered the newborn's eyes, and the voice of the father, who was still looking for the passport and absolutely would not give permission for burial, and dozens of other points of doubt reveal that the ceremony did not go well. And, in addition, there is the word of a person whose name the writer is absolutely not prepared to divulge, since she does not want to deprive anyone of his bread and butter, even if it is earned by washing corpses, which verifies the truth of the saying "Seeing is better than hearing." According to the unknown narrator, when they were taking her to the mortuary (where everyone goes unless they have drowned or have been left suspended in midair in some aerial mishap), the person who was washing her had tried to close the half-closed or half-open eyes of the newborn, but she cunningly prevented it. (It was the first time in her life that she had used any cunning.) The newborn had focused all her might on keeping her eyelids half-open or half-closed, and she had heard the voice of the mortician, which was very like the voices of her sisters, as she complained under her breath: Even your dying has added insult to injury. When the mortician had struggled long with an arm laden with gold bracelets and gotten nowhere, she looked around (something that was completely unnecessary) and punched her hard in the nose (no doubt, if the newborn had had any brains or any presence of mind, she would certainly have wished that when she was seventeen or eighteen, and not in a mortuary but somewhere else, they would have hit her with this punch. Because every big-nose has, with that punch, found its way into the operating room, and, therefore, she could have been relieved of that thing, which was the only worldly means by which, three months after their wedding, the man who was her husband could easily, as with the trunk of an elephant, throw the newborn out of the house just by dragging). In this instant, pain ran through the newborn's body, but she, who always thought that to brush was better than to scream, this time too picked up her toothbrush, laughed under her breath, and said to herself: A punch in the nose is better than a smack in the head.

And then they had taken her to that place everyone knows. They had stretched her out flat in a ditch, and here the newborn had heard the wails of the mourning sisters, who yelled in turn:

"What will we do without you?"

And she was moved, and for the first time in her life she felt guilty, her chest tightened, she stirred in the grave, and her sisters suddenly retreated in horror and pointed at her and shrieked (they shrieked as if they had seen scorpions): "Oh God! She wants to stay alive!"

Here the newborn remembers that she did not know them. And then, naturally, they throw dirt on her, as they throw on everyone; and they put a tombstone on the grave, just as they put tombstones on the graves of others after forty days (in this case especially it can be said, Better safe than sorry). And then the people grip the arms of the sisters who are clad in black and they leave, crying. The newborn—it is unclear where she got so much knowledge—tries to get up and follow them for seven steps, and it is in this instant that her head hits the stone and she regains consciousness and utters her first sentence that is neither strained nor strange: "Ah, how difficult is consciousness."

And then, after that, she starts crying, tears that never end.

Different narrators say that still, after many years, one can hear the sound of her crying from above her grave, and this writer, when she sometimes does not feel like planting beets, goes and sits at the grave to hear that sound.

OCTOBER 1987
TEHRAN
TRANSLATED BY PERSIS KARIM, ATOOSA KOUROSH, PARICHEHR MOIN, DYLAN OEHLER-STRICKLIN, REZA SHIRAZI, AND CATHERINE WILLIAMSON

Three Pictures

1

Lot seventeen, lot twenty-four, and now lot one hundred and twenty-five. It had already reached the foot of the mountains and the government might have to dig the mountainside and place the mounds of corpses that were arriving there until they reached up to the mountain's peak.

The woman rubbed her cheeks quietly and got up. Her gaze glided over the mountains, the mountains that stood tall facing south and stretching their necks toward the western fronts as if waiting for bodies to arrive. A procession of mourners beating themselves on the back with chains was approaching. A mute and lifeless hum, a dusty hum . . .

In front of the line of mourners a man was shouting, loudspeaker in hand, and the tired broken voices were freezing in the air. The man, in order to put some life into the tired, muddy crowd, would clench his fist, wave it in the air, turn to the right and to the left, and shout louder, and the voices, hoarse and stifled, would repeat the words . . .

The children were clutching the wooden handles of the chains tightly and as they got closer to the graves beat themselves harder against their shoulders, proud to be among the adult mourners. The chains left red, swollen marks. The man who led the mourners approached lot one hundred and twenty-five, and as he saw the young, black-clad women, his voice gained new life. He stood in front of the group, pulled up his pants with both hands, and, beating left and right on his chest and sometimes waving his hands toward the crowd to get them going, he sang:

"Mourning, today is mourning, today is a day of mourning . . ."

The stupefied gaze of the women mourners was fixed on the procession. Dried-out cheeks and disheveled hair, lips that had stopped trembling. Petrified statues, petrified, black and distant, removed from what was being chanted, close to what they saw . . . what they had seen, and now no one was wailing, no one's lips were trembling.

The woman, tall and slim, standing in her black veil, looked at the graves that were dug in a row and at the small narrow coffins that were left here and there. On top of a small, narrow coffin the tricolor flag was painted, and the colors had lost their vibrancy. The color white was now gray and the color green rotting, dead and muddy, and it was only the color red that spurted into the eye, as if an artery had been cut or a throat, and the coffin was narrow and light, it easily moved on a tide of blood over the shoulders and was not heavy at all. It was narrow, and no one could fit in it unless he didn't exist, didn't exist at all.

Is it possible for death to change someone that much, make him thin and shrink him so that he would fit in this wooden rectangle . . . ? These wooden boxes are always empty and can be lifted with ease, sliding over hands until they reach a grave, a narrow grave. Empty boxes, empty graves.

She hadn't seen him, and from what she had heard later when she could listen to others:

"The coffin was light, as if only his boots were in there."

And from all that screaming and wailing, she had heard the voice of a woman, unfamiliar, and it was her face that she remembered, two crossed eyes under a black veil:

"Are you alone, woman . . . ? So many thousands have become widows."

"Widow," of all those words scattered in the air, that congealed in her mind and froze; in that black dusty space it was only this word that stayed in her consciousness, and she saw that she was alone, half of her was missing, she was one hand, a hand suspended in the air. Hopeless, waiting for the hand that was lost forever . . . and then they drew her back . . . hands that she didn't know and she saw, she saw hundreds of big black eyes that were staring at her, shaking their heads, with their lips quivering . . . above the graves, near and far they were sitting and only the circles of their faces were visible and the eyes that were red and puffy.

They hadn't let her see him for the last time, her man, her other half, who was tall and square-shouldered, who had black eyes and a childlike laugh! There was nothing in that wooden rectangle . . . there never was anything.

She would come every Thursday. She would come and liked to relive her memories at the side of that cold and unfamiliar stone, the stone under which she didn't know who or what was buried.

When she would get to this part, to this deadly, mysterious doubt, everything would break up in her mind, become confused and elude her. Black eyes, childlike laughter and the height of the man. A man who existed one day and was now a picture in shreds, scattered unrecognizable lines; she couldn't gather them all in one place and make something out of them, an image that she had gotten used to . . . and the more time passed, the more distant it became, the more the lines would scatter . . . The arch of his neck when he turned sideways, the broken line of his side and leg when he was standing and the thin crease created in his shirt and the lines of his cheeks that were lost under his thick black mustache. Broken lines, broken and scattered . . .

For a long time now, she could no longer see him whole— like the first few nights and days, complete and whole, with the uniform of an officer, shining boots and thick mustache. Now even the picture was unfamiliar. As if she didn't know him, something distant, a blue flower that the wind was carrying away, far away . . . She doubted her memories and the photograph, the same one that was above the grave in a glass frame and laughed at her. It was not clear why, why it was laughing, there was nothing funny . . .

The procession of mourners with chains had gone far away, and above a grave some people were unloading a coffin, a woman was wailing:

"I want to see him, I want to look at him."

She covered her ears and closed her eyes so that she

wouldn't hear the voice of the cross-eyed woman who was shouting:

"You aren't the only one, woman . . . so many have become widows."

She knew that a moment later she would faint in some unfamiliar arms, some hand would pull her back, and she, the woman who was wailing, she would see the black puffy eyes with only the hollows of their faces visible under the black veils, and she was afraid to be engraved on the memory of the grieving woman, and pictures, new pictures, push back old pictures and that is why the lines break and get lost and each picture could break a line and mislay it until you doubted the color of your man's eyes . . . was it black or green . . . ?

She passed among the graves and the women who were sitting here and there. The old overhangs were rusted, the overhangs that had been built over the graves several years ago so that the wind and the rain would not destroy the photographs and the mementos of life, but they did, she knew. There was restlessness and distraction and she knew that it wasn't because of the rain and the wind, there was another reason, from within, from the flight of humans toward life. Toward life?

She was walking heedlessly. Heedless of the hands that would sometimes bring a plate of dates from under a chador, and heedless of the voices that she was hearing:

"They say they want to remove all the photographs."

"What for?"

"I don't know, perhaps because of people, the people who come here, after all, so many young men . . ."

"Oh God! Then how are we going to find our graves?"

She was passing among photographs in profile or long shots that were placed in glass frames on metal legs. She stopped before one of the photographs: "Ali at the home of his fiancée (his lover) in Texas."

A big white house and a green lawn, Ali with his hands on his hips among the greenery, and where is the girl? Does she even know or doesn't she remember anymore? Most probably she has forgotten. Time has a quicker pace there and crushes everything and doesn't let you pause and search everywhere for broken lines until you yourself don't know whether he existed at all, and there everything is summarized into the shape of a postcard and then a look, a smile . . . This Ali was Iranian . . . Persian . . . Persian, and now in his country . . . far, he lives in a faraway place. Lives . . . ?

She pulled up the edge of the chador on her head and passed by the photograph and the pictures, pictures that were losing color . . . A martyr is the heart of history . . . We who stand tall are the constants of history.

And this young man next to a used Zhiyan car and this boy who has a band on his forehead with a sweet smile on his lips and a gun in his hand.

She stopped in front of a new picture, the top of the grave was wet, wet with water, and she read its date, it wasn't too long ago, only two months. A young man in a karate uniform clenching his fists in midair as if he wanted to come out of the glass and smash everything to pieces. His jaws tight, his lips pursed and his brow knotted in a frown, and his mouth that was open in a shout, and what was he saying? In what tongue was he shouting that no one could hear his voice . . . ? And if cries are soundless, like all the cries that she was hearing and had heard.

The sun was setting and the tree branches were shrouded in a nightmarish red. Tired mourners were getting up from beside the graves, women were shaking their black chadors, the sound of the procession of mourners was no longer there, and in the sky a flock of crows was flying toward the red glow of the sunset.

She was lost among the crowd, voices, voices of tired people who were leaving the cemetery ringing in her head.

"Behesht-e Zahra Cemetery will be closed for one week."

"Why?"

"They are coming from Turkey to see the Fountain of the Martyrs."

"Then what about those who become martyrs this week, what should they do?"

"They have to go to the morgue and stay there until the Turkish delegation leaves."

"Does that mean it will be closed on Thursday, too?"

"Well . . . I suppose."

"God! What should we do about Thursday and Friday?"

2

The man was shouting at the top of his lungs:

"Half the price you pay in town, half the price you pay in town."

The mourners, dusty and tired, were coming out of Behesht-e Zahra Cemetery. The gate to the cemetery was spitting everybody out like a big mouth. Women with black, muddy chadors were walking slowly and heavily, like the dead having risen from the grave, to the other side of the road. Sacks of potatoes and onions were being emptied one by one. The passage of cars was cutting into the long line of those who were crossing the road. The salesman was shouting:

"Come and get it, come and get it, half the price you pay in town." It was cheap. Everything. And the women were bumping against each other, grabbing the corner of each other's chadors and shouting at one another, "There's a line, lady . . . get out of the way, kid; you just got here, mister."

And there was a line, a long black line, and hungry fearful eyes and the sacks that were getting emptied and the bags that were being filled and the salesman who was changing the weights on the scale continuously.

The man was sweating, he would wave toward the people who were coming out of the big gate with his hands, his muddied hands, and he would shout:

"Half the price you pay in town . . ."

Then he would scratch behind his ears, bend over the scale, and keep on loading and unloading it.

"If you give it to me for nine tomans a kilo, I'll buy a sack."

The buyer was a fat man with a red chubby face and a thick Turkish accent; haggling with the salesman, he would turn and look at the women in the line every now and then and laugh; he had two gold teeth and was shifting in his place, and he was happy, very happy.

The buyer dragged away the sack of potatoes, and the salesman changed the weight:

"How many kilos, sister . . . ?"

"Three kilos . . ."

The salesman's frown and the three-kilo weight that he put

on the scale and the fat man who had become even redder and was still pulling the sack looked her up and down and his gold teeth flashed:

"Are you taking it for a cat, lady . . . ?"

She pulled her chador down over her forehead, took the bag of potatoes, and started toward the road. Double-deck buses leaning from too many passengers were tumbling toward the city, black heads of women and children who were staring out of the windows, two palms glued to the window, and carefree eyes, carefree and empty of memories, and how nice that they are at the onset of absorbing images and memories, how nice and how awful . . . Too bad they finally grow tall and have their pictures taken in the air with combat uniforms or next to a Zhiyan car, and it must be taken, the picture must be taken, that moment when you laugh and then forget that you had laughed and what for.

It was getting dark. The buyer had started his green BMW. He didn't have any passengers.

The man pressed his foot on the gas pedal and the car took off.

3

"For God's sake, sir, a little slower . . ."

The man's gold teeth flashed in a smirk:

"Are you afraid of dying?"

The woman used the chador to hide her face. The man couldn't see it.

"You didn't answer, are you afraid of dying?"

The woman sighed deeply:

"No! But to die for nothing . . ."

The man laughed loudly, shook his head, and hit the wheel forcefully.

"For nothing . . . for nothing, I myself don't want to die for nothing."

The woman did not comment and stared out the window. The light drizzle that had started and would certainly fall on the coffins, could it make the colors colorful, turn white into white and green into green and the color red? No, it becomes redder, when it rains it creates small streams of blood . . .

from inside the ditches, the cut arteries and severed hands and feet and the blood that would never stop, and these Thursdays that always are, this rain that has always been, and black-clad women and leaning buses. How about before all this, a long time ago, when Behesht-e Zahra Cemetery wasn't Behesht-e Zahra Cemetery, what did she do, where was she, and where did she used to go on Thursdays?

She didn't used to go anywhere and there wasn't anything on her mind except a cloudy sky and the graves that were continuously filled up and the land that was continuously dug up. It seemed that ever since childhood, from the time when she had an unaffected memory-free mind, she had only come and gone on this same path. This rough and strange path with tall trees and green tops of wheat fields that would be harvested eventually and the crows that were flying care-free in a cloudy sky and the army of mourners riding in different vehicles.

She jerked forward with the braking of the buyer and fearfully looked around. The buyer was laughing:

"Ma'am, you're too nervous. How long has your husband been dead?"

The woman said:

"How did you know?"

"Know what, ma'am?"

"That my husband is dead."

"It wasn't hard, ma'am, you don't look as though it could have been your son killed, so it must have been your husband, ma'am . . . How many months has it been since it happened, ma'am?"

"Nine months."

The buyer's face tightened, he wetted his lips with his tongue, like the time when he was buying the potatoes and the woman saw that the young karate man was suspended in the air with clenched fists and the shout that no one could hear and through the fog above the road he was coming toward them.

"May he rest in peace, ma'am, but the dirt of the grave is cold, one gets used to it."

The woman turned her face away and slowly muttered, "No," and saw that the face of the young karate man had tightened and he was shouting and he couldn't reach them, reach the car's windshield, and was left in that same way, suspended in midair.

"Listen to me, ma'am, you don't bury yourself with the dead . . . so, you probably come here every week."

She took a sideways glance at him, he was forty years old with strong full cheeks, why would he come, with his skin glowing so?

"What about you? Do you come here every week?"

The man gave a short laugh, started rapping on the wheel with two fingers:

"Every week, ma'am, right on time; if it were possible I would come on other days as well."

"Your relative must have died a long time ago."

"As a matter of fact, all my relatives are alive, ma'am . . ."

The buyer laughed loudly.

A loud shout echoed through the air and the woman looked straight ahead, it was the young karate man who was shouting, waving his fists, and couldn't reach the windshield of the car. The woman pulled herself together, slid toward the car's door, and saw a dark blue Renault on the right side; she was mesmerized for a moment. She hurriedly rolled down the window and looked out, behind the wheel there was an old man with a thick white beard who was slouched down with tears on his cheeks and an old woman next to him and three young women in the back; the third one had rolled down the window like her and was looking out and perhaps was searching for a Renault that was dark blue with a young man whose face was softly, calmly fading sitting behind the wheel and was perhaps remembering that every morning she used to stand behind the window until her man blew the horn from the end of the alley and waved to her before disappearing.

It was foggy and the cars were disappearing into the fog, as did the dark blue Renault, and the woman looked and saw that the karate man was still coming toward them and heard the voice of the buyer, who, as if he hadn't heard the shouts of the young man and had only seen the dark blue Renault, said: "All these are the wives of the martyrs."

The woman was still silent and saw that something was

wriggling in the hand of the young karate man, she bent forward and looked closer, it seemed to be a piece of a picture, a piece of her husband's picture, two black eyes, black and huge.

"After a time everybody forgets; you'll forget, too. If you don't believe it you can ask the old-timers."

It was the voice of the buyer and the woman had only heard the word "ask" and was now looking at him, perplexed: "Ask what?"

"About how they forget, must forget, it is a sin . . ."

The buyer laughed loudly and the woman pressed herself against the car door, and in the fog she saw thousands of young karate men with something in their hands coming toward her, pieces of a picture, a picture of a man in an officer's uniform . . . and those, if those pieces of photographs don't reach one another and remain suspended in the air forever like this?

The buyer said: "Don't be afraid, ma'am, don't worry."

It seemed as if a wind was separating the young karate men and they, facing the wind, were trying to reach one another and complete something in midair in front of the woman, something that was in shreds, and now the wind was howling and blowing them apart and they were going up as if they were flying, up above the wind and the whirlwind that had started, they were going to join one another and complete the photograph, the photograph of an officer with big black eyes.

The woman thought that one word, only one word uttered by her, would settle that whirlwind and now not for the picture that she wanted to be completed, but for their sake, those young karate men who were wandering in the air and were shouting, whose fists were clenched in the empty air, it was for their sake that she wanted the wind to stop and the whirlwind . . .

"I am a teacher, sir, you know?"

"Well, you don't need money, thank God."

The wind was calming down. The young karate men were reaching one another; her husband's picture was being completed. The woman held her veil under her neck tightly, only her face was visible and eyes that were now calm and no longer frightened . . .

"My husband was an officer . . ."

They had reached the curve near the slaughterhouse, the man looked at her.

"I have some experience, ma'am, sooner or later everybody gets used to it."

The woman smirked, the man pulled himself together and turned onto the street, a crowded street with car horns blowing continuously, and sheep that were marked in different colors on the sidewalk. Colors of blue, red, black. The woman was silently watching; the man as if following her eyes slowly murmured:

"They are marked so they don't get mixed up, you understand; sheep are sheep, only their owners are different!"

As she got out of the car, she took out some money and held it out toward the man. He smirked:

"I don't have any change, ma'am."

Heedlessly, the woman dropped the money on the seat, the young karate man was still shouting and the picture was pointing the way home.

SUMMER 1986
TEHRAN
TRANSLATED BY PARICHEHR MOIN

Milton Keynes UK
Ingram Content Group UK Ltd.
UKHW040722291023
431426UK00013B/276